Undercover Cook
Jeannie Watt

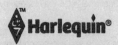

TORONTO NEW YORK LONDON
AMSTERDAM PARIS SYDNEY HAMBURG
STOCKHOLM ATHENS TOKYO MILAN MADRID
PRAGUE WARSAW BUDAPEST AUCKLAND

Recycling programs
for this product may
not exist in your area.

ISBN-13: 978-0-373-71755-2

UNDERCOVER COOK

www.Harlequin.com

Printed in U.S.A.

"I can learn by watching."

Eden, their cooking instructor, set a clean skillet on the counter in front of him. "Use this pan. Cook some eggs. Make your grandfather happy."

Gabe gave a soft snort as Nick started stirring his eggs in the bowl. A few minutes later, the old man said, "You know, Eden's cute."

"Yeah."

Gabe tapped the spoon on the side of the bowl. "Aren't you ever going to start looking again?"

Nick sucked in a breath. It'd been two years since he'd lost his wife in a car wreck. And no, he hadn't started looking again. "This isn't the time to discuss this, Granddad."

"When is?"

Nick shook his head and reached for another egg. He cracked it on the side of the counter and the whole damned thing exploded in his hand, splattering yolk on his shirt and pants.

"Thin-shelled egg," Eden said from behind him. "They need to feed the chickens more calcium."

"Good to know," Nick said, looking down at the yolk spots. Eden smiled at him and he smiled back... wondering what it would take to get her to trust him.

While she began talking to her gathered students, Nick pretended to listen. Which of those closed doors across the room might hold a computer? he wondered. There was a computer in the front reception area, but he doubted it was linked to financial accounts. He would check it out, though.

When he got the chance.

Dear Reader,

Have you ever heard the old saying, "What a tangled web we weave, when first we practice to deceive?" Detective Nick Duncan hadn't planned on tangling webs when he joined Eden Tremont's cooking class. All he wanted was the quickest way possible to discover if Tremont Catering was involved in laundering drug money. Unfortunately, thanks to the efforts of an enthusiastic member of his investigative team, he ends up masquerading as a home security expert and actively deceiving the first woman he's been interested in since losing his wife.

Trust is paramount to Eden Tremont after being raised by a father who made promises he never kept and recently discovering that her ex-boyfriend was a serial cheater. Nick Duncan, the man who's installing her home security system seems utterly trustworthy, but after Eden starts to fall for him, she discovers all is not as it seems.

The challenge of writing this story was to keep Nick's character sympathetic as he actively deceived the heroine. He had good reasons for what he did, but as time passed, he became less and less certain that the end justified the means—especially when he was bending the law himself. Eden had to come to terms with her trust issues and decide if the man she'd fallen for was the real Nick Duncan.

I hope you enjoy reading *Undercover Cook*, which is the second of my three-book series, Too Many Cooks? I'd love to hear from you at jeanniewrites@gmail.com or via my website, www.jeanniewatt.com.

Best wishes,

Jeannie Watt

ABOUT THE AUTHOR

Jeannie Watt lives off the grid in rural Nevada and loves nothing better than an excellent meal. Jeannie is blessed with a husband who cooks more than she does, a son who knows how to make tapas and a daughter who knows the best restaurants in San Francisco. Her idea of heaven is homemade macaroni and cheese.

Books by Jeannie Watt

HARLEQUIN SUPERROMANCE

*Too Many Cooks?

Other titles by this author available in ebook

To Jake, my consultant in kitchen and cop matters.
Thank you.

CHAPTER ONE

"COOKING LESSONS?" Detective Daphne Sparks paused with her coffee halfway to her lips and made an are-you-kidding face. "We have a missing, probably dead, informant, and your solution is cooking lessons?"

"Dumb idea," Marcus Jethro echoed from across the table.

Nick Duncan kept his eyes on Daphne, his partner, because if he looked at Marcus he was going to say something he regretted.

"It's simple," he said. "I go with Granddad to the lessons at the catering kitchen, get the layout, figure out how best to get at the company financial records." And from those, determine whether Tremont Catering, based in Reno, was laundering Lake Tahoe drug money. As he'd said. Simple.

He pushed his chair back slightly to make room for his legs under the small table in the back corner of a Virginia Street deli—the place where he and Daphne usually met for lunch in the late afternoon, after the noon-hour crowd was gone and they could talk.

"How is it that the lessons happen to be at this particular kitchen?" Daphne asked mildly, pushing long black hair over her shoulders. Nick shrugged. "I see," she said, lifting her coffee cup in a small salute.

"Any information you get that way is totally inadmissible," Marcus interjected in a superior tone, before adding a carefully measured half tea-spoon of sugar to his coffee. He hated to be left out, and since he was a forensic accountant for the Reno PD, and because of that usually chained to his desk, he often was. Marcus had visions of crime-fighting glory that weren't quite working out.

"I'm not going to seize the records," Nick said. "I'm going to examine them, see if we're wasting time on something that isn't going to pan out."

He and Daphne had been working for months as Reno PD members of the Washoe-Tahoe Drug Task Force, trying to get a toehold into the drug traffic moving through the Tahoe Summit Hotel and Casino. They knew kitchen personnel were involved, and they'd gotten some indication of how the money might be moving. But task-force funds were spread so thinly that after eight fruitless months of investigation, the Tahoe Summit had been shoved to the back burner...despite the fact that Nick and Daphne's twenty-one-year-old confidential informant, Cully, had recently gone missing. Nick thought that circumstance warranted further investigation. His lieutenant had disagreed. Strongly.

"I don't like it," Marcus said.

It didn't matter if he liked it, because Nick didn't answer to him. Technically, since his asshole lieutenant had suspended him for thirty days after their heated "discussion," Nick didn't answer to anyone in the department, which was why his investigation into Tremont Catering fell into the unofficial category. His own time, his own dime. But how the hell else was he supposed to get the answers he needed, not only to work on the drug trafficking, but to find out what had happened to Cully?

"What do *you* suggest?" he finally asked Marcus, more to mollify him than anything. They needed his expertise once Nick got copies of the financial records.

The accountant rolled his shoulders and then took on a thoughtful expression while slowly stirring his coffee. "If you decide to go with the cooking-lesson angle, you could use it as a means to conduct an indirect investigation and try to determine if there are indications of expenditures exceeding legal income. Then go before a judge and ask for a warrant."

"And perhaps wait for a glacier to melt in the process?" Nick asked.

Marcus flushed. "It's the only course of action that will lead to admissible evidence."

"Look," Nick said. "I understand admissibility. And I don't like doing things this way, but I also don't want to waste time." He stabbed his fork into a bowl of ravioli, spearing one and holding it poised in the air. "I don't need to make a formal case. All I need is enough information to get Justin Tremont to roll and give me names if he's involved."

"And if he isn't?" Marcus asked, putting the spoon on a napkin.

"Then we're at a dead end. For now."

In Nick's last discussion with Cully, the CI had indicated that Tahoe Summit drug money was being laundered through a small Reno business. He'd sounded excited when he'd called to set up a meeting, and Nick had been relieved to finally get a break in the case. Chasing dirty money often resulted in a bust.

But Cully never showed for the meeting. Or

called. Suspecting the worst, Nick and Daphne had started digging into small businesses connected with Tahoe Summit personnel. It hadn't taken long to discover that only one person on the kitchen staff had ties to a small business. Justin Tremont, part-time pastry chef, owned a catering business with his two sisters.

Marcus shook his head. "Risky. My way may take time, but at least you won't end up getting investigated by Internal Affairs."

"That won't happen," Nick said.

"You hope." Daphne eyed him over the top of her coffee cup.

"Stop being such a ray of sunshine," he muttered.

"I vote against this idea," Marcus said, pushing his lank dark hair to the side of his forehead.

"You don't have a vote," Nick said.

"When you want me to look at the figures, you might change your mind on that."

"All right, you have a vote. But it's still two against one."

"Marcus," Daphne said, fixing her large, coffee-brown eyes on his face in a way that told Nick she was on her last nerve. Marcus was, of course, oblivious. "I have sworn to uphold the law. I truly believe in the law, but I want to get the sons of bitches that nailed Cully. Don't you?"

"Of course I want to get them," the accountant said adamantly. He wanted anything that Daphne wanted—he'd had a wild crush on her since he'd first come to work two years ago.

"Then man up!" she said, and Marcus went instantly red.

"Fine," he sputtered. "I'll man up. I'm more than capable of bending the rules."

"You don't need to bend anything," Nick said. "All we want is your unofficial expertise after I get the financial records in an unofficial way. All right?"

Marcus was still red. He shot a quick look at Daphne who stared back impassively. "Yes. All right. But I'm not the dweeb you think I am."

"No one said you were a dweeb," Nick insisted, since Daphne wouldn't. She had no patience with their colleague and Nick couldn't blame her, since Marcus was hell-bent on impressing her and impervious to hints—or blatant declarations—that she wasn't interested.

"You don't have to say it," the accountant said sullenly. "I can see what you think."

Daphne dropped her napkin onto her plate, obviously having had enough. She reached for her purse, took out a handful of one-dollar bills and started counting them.

"What are you going to do now?" Nick asked.

"I am going to take my partnerless self back to the office to work on busting drug buys near the campus. Because it looks good in the newspaper." She raised her eyes. "I don't care how much of a jerk Lieutenant Davidson is, don't ever do this to me again."

Nick pulled a twenty from his wallet. "I'll try very hard to never rile him again."

Frankly, he wasn't normally the lieutenant-riling kind, but this Cully deal bugged the hell out of him. Yeah, Cully had been slick, but he'd also been a sweet, personable kid, with plans, no less. Both Nick and Daphne had, during weak moments, mentioned that as much as they appreciated what he brought them, he needed to find a safer line of work.

Cully had laughed them off, saying that he was eventually going to Police Officer Standard and Training academy to become a professional undercover agent, and this was good practice. He wouldn't have gone to ground without contacting either Daphne or Nick, and it had now been four weeks since they'd last heard from him.

EDEN TREMONT KICKED off the killer heels she wore to all her client meetings the instant she stepped inside the back door of the catering kitchen. She sighed as her bare feet hit the blessedly cool tile floor, then reached for her orange kitchen clogs. It didn't pay to be short.

Sunday-morning meetings were not the norm for her. Usually she spent that time prepping meals for the two families she cooked for on a weekly basis—the Stewarts and the Ballards—in addition to her catering duties. Today, however, was the only time a prospective bride with a vicious travel schedule could meet with her, and Eden went with it. Happily so, since she had a signed contract in her hand.

No one was in the kitchen yet, so she stowed her portfolio and her purse in the small back office. Grabbing an elastic band off the top of her desk, she pulled her blond hair into a haphazard knot and secured it just as the rear door of the kitchen banged open, scaring the bejeezus out of her. Patty Lloyd, their prep cook, did not slam. Ever.

Then one of the lockers next to the back door rattled and Eden let out a breath.

Justin. Her brother. Who wasn't supposed to be in until the early afternoon.

"Why are you here now?" Eden demanded, leaning out the door.

"Guess." Justin barely held back a yawn before pulling a white, jersey-cotton stocking cap over his choppy blond hair. Sometimes Eden wondered if he still cut it himself, as he had when they were kids. It wasn't that he couldn't afford a haircut. He was just never able to find a barber who could give him the dangerous skater-punk do he wanted.

"You took a cake order when you shouldn't have?" Her voice dripped sisterly sarcasm.

"Hey, you're one to talk. You volunteered to help with geriatric cooking lessons when you're swamped."

"I'm not as swamped as you, I have help with the lessons and it's only for six weeks." She folded her arms. "Besides, it's community service and that's not only great for the soul, it's excellent public relations." She cocked her head, scowling at her brother. Sometimes she honestly worried about him. "How late did you get in last night?"

Justin shrugged into a chef's jacket with a blue-food-color stain dribbled down the front. His favorite jacket. He said it unleashed his creativity. "Two? Two-thirty?"

"So you got what? Three hours sleep?"

"I'm too tired to do the math," he said as he headed past her to one of the two stainless-steel fridges and pulled open the door. A weary smile transformed his angular face as he glanced over his shoulder at Eden. "Did I tell you that I love Patty? That I'm going to make her my bride?" He pulled out a stainless-steel bowl of what had to be cake filling, and held it up. "One less thing to do. If I play my cards right, I may be able to sneak in a nap before I head back up to the Lake." The Lake being shorthand for Lake Tahoe, where Justin had his second job.

By day, Justin was the Tremont Catering dessert chef, but he also worked three nights a week at a Lake Tahoe resort hotel as the pastry chef, and, in spite of those two jobs filling much of his time, he kept making high-end cakes. The more he made, the more the orders poured in as word spread. And they all seemed to be rush jobs. If they weren't to begin with, then by the time Justin fit them into his jammed schedule, they became rushes.

"You've got to stop doing this," Eden muttered. Her words were barely audible, since she knew they would do no good. She'd been saying the same thing over and over again for how long now? Since he'd taken that first emergency cake order for a bakery that'd had an electrical fire.

Even on that first order he'd been pushing things. They'd had three big catering events that week, yet he'd still somehow pulled off a masterpiece. And Eden knew the argument she'd get in return—the cakes brought in a lot of extra income. Some old equipment had finally been replaced, thanks to those cakes, and Justin had been able to refurbish the classic Firebird he'd bought from one of Eden's clients. Plus he was socking away money to make a balloon payment on his condo.

At some point all this was going to catch up to him—physically, if nothing else—even if he did have Patty. When, exactly, had she made the filling? She was supposed to have gone home shortly after Eden left. Obviously, she hadn't. Their prep cook needed to be needed, and with their sister, Reggie, out on maternity leave, and Justin's ridiculous schedule, Patty was working at the right place.

"When's this cake due?" Eden asked as she started breading beef for stew. She made five days of container meals for the Stewarts and the Ballards every Sunday and delivered them late Sunday evening. During the remainder of the week, between catering events and prep, she planned menus and typed up reheating instructions, which she saved to her computer for repeat performances. She had the personal-chef gig down to a fine science now.

"Tomorrow," Justin said. "I have Donovan coming over to help me deliver."

"Then I can have the van tonight?"

"All yours," Justin agreed.

"Great." Eden hated delivering in her small Honda Civic.

"Am I making crème brûlée for the Wednesday deal?"

"Yes. And mini tarts."

"Got it." Justin disappeared back into the alcove known as the pastry cave, and turned on his music. Eden chopped vegetables in time to classic Green Day songs as she browned the sausages for the lasagna the Ballard family requested as a weekly staple. Easy for two teenage boys to fill up on.

By the time Patty came in at eight-thirty, Eden had every burner on the stove going, as well as two ovens. She tended to hog the kitchen on Sunday, which was why they avoided Monday events if at all possible. Today was officially

Patty's day off, so she would be coming in for only one reason....

"Good morning," she said, pulling a scarf from her permed curls. "I thought I'd stop by and see if Justin needed some help."

"You know he does," Eden said. "How late were you here last night?"

"Only until eight, but I didn't put down the extra hours. It was my choice to stay."

"Put down the hours," Eden said. "It comes out of the cake money, since that's what you were here for."

"If you insist," Patty said. "Even though I'm happy—"

"I insist. But, really, you shouldn't stay late to help Justin out of situations he gets himself into."

"It's for the good of the company."

"Yes." Hard to argue with that.

"The oddest thing happened last night," Patty said as she tied on her oversize apron. "When I went out to my car, there was a young man hanging out in the alley near the van."

Eden looked up from the carrots she was dicing. "Just...hanging around? Loitering?"

Their Reno neighborhood was a quiet one, consisting of a couple small bistro-type restaurants that were open only for breakfast and lunch, law offices and boutique stores in refurbished houses and a quiet, upscale lounge two blocks away. They didn't get many people lingering after hours—especially in their alley, which was a dead-end.

"Yes. I thought it was strange, but I just walked straight to my car, got in and locked the doors. Once I had it started, I checked and saw the man slipping into the space between our building and the law office, apparently on his way to the street. When I pulled out of the alley, he was gone. Or he may have been hiding between the buildings."

"Any chance it was—"

"It wasn't Ian," Patty said in a definite voice, referring to Eden's ex-boyfriend.

"Hey, Justin?" Eden called, loudly enough to be heard over the music. Her brother came out of the pastry room, stainless-steel spatula in hand. "Patty said there was someone hanging around the van last night when she left. Maybe you should take a look at it, see if he tried to pry the doors open or something."

"Yeah. Sure." He put the spatula down on the counter nearest him and headed for the back door. "Any chance it was Ian?"

"Patty says it wasn't," Eden answered wearily.

A few minutes later he was back. "Nothing.

Maybe just a homeless guy looking for a place to sleep."

"Probably," Patty agreed.

"But maybe you should park out front on the days you're working late," Eden said. "And keep an eye on your surroundings, all right?"

Patty sniffed. She was the designated lecturer.

"For your safety," Eden added. Ever since Reggie—her and Justin's older sister—had started maternity leave, Patty had all but declared herself a full partner in Tremont Catering. Granted, they needed her. She was dependable and honest, and without her Justin would be in deep trouble. But she did have a few quirks, control issues being at the top of the list.

"I'll watch myself," she said. "And I *am* positive it wasn't Ian. This man had dark hair."

Eden gave a quick nod of understanding before she walked into the dry storage area. She hated that Patty was so aware Ian would be her number-one suspect. Eden very much liked to keep her private life private. It was her own fault, though, that Patty was so well-informed on the ex-boyfriend front, since Eden had taken a strip off his cheating hide when he'd had the audacity to show up at the kitchen with flowers and an apology, delivered with the perfect combination of sincerity and humility.

Eden hadn't budged, and after a few words it became clear that he didn't think coming on to Vanessa, his best friend's wife, in the guest bedroom at a dinner party counted as cheating. He had, after all, been drunk, and they hadn't done anything but a little kissing and groping. It was all a big misunderstanding. Surely Eden could see that? His friend understood, so why didn't she? Shattering her trust? No big deal. Being drunk? Hell of an excuse.

Eden dragged the stepladder from one end of the metal shelving units to the other and started climbing so she could get two large cans of fire-roasted crushed tomatoes. After a stressful childhood with a father who said anything to keep people happy, then did as he damned well pleased, she had no tolerance for subterfuge, lying or "misunderstandings." Which was why she didn't care how many bouquets of flowers or apologies Ian sent her way.

They'd dated once before and he'd left her, shortly after college. It'd taken her a long time to get over him. When he'd appeared back in Reno six months ago, he'd come to see her. Apologized for being such a short-sighted jerk. Asked her back into his life. Eden had taken a chance, thinking they'd both grown and that Ian had dealt with whatever issue had caused him to leave her in the first place.

And the flame had burned hot.

Now, thanks to him, it had abruptly gone out, and that was it. Over was over, and he needed to get that through his thick head.

Unfortunately, Ian hated to lose. That probably made him a good lawyer. It also made him a pain in the ass.

Amazing just how quickly things changed once a person discovered that the guy who was supposed to be watching her back was actually more interested in someone else's boobs.

"WHAT DO YOU mean, you aren't taking the cooking lessons?" Nick stared at his stubborn grandfather, who stood next to the patio door of his small apartment wearing his favorite plaid flannel shirt and baggy police tactical pants. A couple quail ran across the courtyard lawn outside.

Gabe pulled the door open. The quail instantly took cover in a juniper bush. "Why in the hell would I want to take cooking lessons?" he asked as he grabbed the bag of seeds off the bookcase by the door.

Because I want to take them.

"Lois says you guys need to eat better. This is one way to do that."

"I'm eating just fine."

"You're downing too much salt and fat. She said your blood pressure has redlined a couple times. If you don't start eating right, she's going to sentence you to the cafeteria."

"When did this happen?" Gabe asked, shaking his head before reaching into the bag and tossing a handful of seeds out into the grass.

"What?"

"When did I hit the point in my life when I have to be treated like a damned child?" He didn't look at Nick, just threw more seeds, his movements jerky. Angry.

Nick didn't have an answer for that. His grandfather was a seventy-five-year-old heart-attack survivor. After the heart attack it became apparent that living alone in his north Reno home was no longer a possibility, so Nick had helped him sell the house and move into the Candlewood Center, an assisted-living facility that would allow him the most personal freedom. It cost a bundle, but Gabe had made a huge profit on the house, which allowed him to pay the fees and still have money in the bank.

Not a bad outcome, except for the part where Gabe resented being told what to do.

He did okay with community living, and had made several friends. But while he happily played poker, took the weekly trip to the golf course, sat in front of the huge TV and ate low-sodium popcorn while watching sports with his friends, he steadfastly refused to partake in the meal plan offered by the facility.

After Gabe had balked, so had a couple of his new buddies. Their rebellion was driving the woman in charge of health care in Gabe's block of apartments crazy as their blood pressures inched up. Fortunately, Lois was no pushover and had come up with this cooking-lesson angle as a way to get the guys to eat healthier meals.

And when she'd mentioned her plan to Nick— in hopes that he'd convince his grandfather, the ringleader, to cooperate—he'd had the happy suggestion that perhaps she'd like to contact Tremont Catering, which was less than a mile away, and see if they could rent their large kitchen for the lessons. It made more sense than trying to squeeze all the participants into the relatively tiny cafeteria kitchen at the facility.

The only downside was that instead of simply

renting the kitchen, the Tremonts had insisted on being involved with the lessons. Nick would have preferred to have the place to himself, in order to snoop around while Lois did her thing, but this was definitely better than nothing.

"I'm not going to live forever," Gabe said, pushing the door shut. Little quail heads appeared out of the juniper. "But while I am alive, I want to eat decent food."

"That's what the class is all about. Taking stuff you love and making it healthier."

"Making it taste like cardboard, you mean. Your grandmother went on a health-food craze once. Let me tell you, that stuff she made with those *healthy*—" Gabe's mouth twisted into a disdainful sneer "—recipes was awful. And you know your grandmother was a damned fine cook."

Nick's grandparents had divorced long before Nick had been born and Gabe rarely talked about the woman who'd left him. It was interesting that he appreciated what a fine cook she'd been. "Things have changed." Nick assumed they'd changed, anyway.

He knew nothing about cooking, other than frying up the occasional steak. Everything he ate came from the freezer or a take-out bag.

"I was kind of hoping you'd take the lessons for my sake."

"Your sake?" Gabe sounded surprised, then his expression shifted. "There's no possibility that an attractive woman might be teaching these lessons, is there?"

Not that again.

Nick toyed with the idea of simply saying yes, but heaven only knew what his grandfather would do then. Nightmare scenarios shot through his head.

Nick's wife, Miri, had died more than two years ago in a car accident and Gabe, who'd adored her, had grieved along with Nick. But after a year and a half had passed and Nick had remained buried in his work, with no social life and showing no sign of changing his ways, his grandfather had grown impatient. It was time for Nick to move on, "join the land of the living" as Gabe put it.

Nick was in the land of the living; he'd finally gotten over the raw pain of losing his wife, but he felt no desire whatsoever to try to fill the void she'd left in his life. Yes, the void was dark and unfulfilling, but it didn't hurt. Why fill it with something that might cause him pain later?

"I want to learn some cooking techniques,

Granddad," he said in an exasperated voice. "Not flirt with the instructor."

Gabe's mouth twisted in annoyance. "Take your own damned lessons, then. Leave me out of it."

"Darn it, Granddad. Stop being so effing stubborn."

"Effing? In my day, we just came out and said—"

"I'm trying to be polite."

"Why aren't you at work?" Gabe suddenly asked.

Nick rolled his eyes. He wasn't going to explain about his tool of a lieutenant or the reason he'd been suspended. For one thing, it was embarrassing. For another, Gabe would want every detail leading up to the suspension, and Nick wasn't discussing the matter. Nick did not have a short fuse, but he'd been hot with the lieutenant. A little too hot. He honestly had a soft spot for the kid who'd been feeding them information and had then so abruptly disappeared. Wanted to look into the matter instead of having it shoved onto the back burner in favor of easier and more high-profile cases—such as busting drugs near the campus. Maybe they hadn't made much headway in eight months, but in light of what had happened, pulling them entirely off the case made no sense, either.

"Different assignment, different hours," he said dismissively. Gabe narrowed his eyes thoughtfully and Nick was suddenly reminded of all the times he'd unsuccessfully tried to pull a fast one on the old guy when he'd been a kid. "Come on, Granddad. Take the lessons. I want you to join, since I know jack about cooking, and I can't if you don't."

"You want to take the lessons? You want to learn to make old-people food?"

"I want to learn to cook something healthy so I don't end up having a heart attack."

Gabe scowled at him, then shoved a hand through his thick white hair. "That's dirty pool."

"Only two of the guys have signed up, but more will if you do. And I honestly want to go."

Gabe grunted, setting the birdseed bag down on the small table next to the window. "Sign me the hell up, then. You're not going to rest until you do."

"No. I'm not. It's a win-win."

Gabe then said the word that Nick had avoided in the name of politeness.

NICK WANTED TO take cooking lessons? Ha. Nick wanted to maneuver his grandfather into doing something he didn't want to do and wasn't above using emotional blackmail. Gabe still wasn't quite sure why he'd let himself get wrangled into these lessons, except that it was obvious Nick had an ulterior motive and Gabe was curious as to what it was. Too bad it wasn't the one he'd suggested—a cute teacher his grandson wanted to get to know.

Nick had changed since his wife had died. Drawn into himself, which was to be expected under the circumstances, and thrown himself into his work to deal with the grief. But after two years, he was still withdrawn, still totally focused on work and nothing but work, which worried Gabe.

He'd done the same back in his prime, after his wife had left him. And the result had not been good—in fact it had cost him dearly—and now here he was, alone, stuck in an old folks' home. And he didn't even have any decent memories to keep him company. The only thing that helped was that he was with some of his own kind. Lenny Hartman, the old son of a bitch, had been in law enforcement down in Vegas, and Paul Meyer had been a firefighter until he retired.

Both men had checked into Candlewood voluntarily, after their wives had passed away, something Gabe would never understand. He'd hung on to his independence until the last possible moment—where it was either Candlewood or Nick moving in with him after the heart attack. Nick had offered. Gabe had declined. His grandson needed to be in a position to get on with his life, and living with a cranky grandfather was not conducive to bringing home a hot woman.

Gabe walked over to his computer and brought up a screen, pleased that he was feeling a lot more comfortable using the contraption. For years he'd put off learning to use one, had allowed himself to be intimidated even though Nick had given him a laptop, until that damned Lois had forced him and the other guys into taking a basic class just a few months ago.

He couldn't remember seeing a more intimidated group of men than he and his fellow inmates when they'd first settled in front of the computer screens at the community-college technology lab. Lenny's first official act had been to pour coffee over his keyboard by "accident," only to find that all the instructor had to do was unplug that keyboard, set it out to dry and plug in another.

After that they decided resistance was futile

and discovered, grudgingly, that, yes, a computer could change a guy's life. Open his world.

Make it seem less like he was in stir.

Gabe sat in his chair—an ergonomic model Nick had given him for Christmas instead of the recliner he really wanted, a blatant effort to get him to learn to use the laptop. He had to admit, though, that he liked the chair and because of it spent more hours on the computer than he had ever expected.

Which was how he knew that Nick didn't even have a Facebook page. How in the hell was he going to socialize if he didn't have the gumption to sign up for a social network?

Somehow Gabe had to come up with a way to kick his grandson in the ass and make him get on with his life—to not make the same damned mistakes Gabe had made in the name of professional achievement.

And fear.

CHAPTER TWO

EDEN TOOK A moment to survey her class: seven men of varying shapes and sizes, their ages ranging from sixty to eighty, and two younger guys. One of the latter was tall and thin, with a pale complexion, dark hair and a know-it-all expression. The other, standing next to an elderly man with an almost identical jaw and nose, was taller, broader, and also dark haired. Every now and then he would cut his eye toward the first young guy and frown slightly.

Tall, sturdy Lois, who had first contacted Eden about renting the kitchen, hovered at the periphery, keeping a close eye on her charges. During their initial conversation she had admitted that her own cooking skills were closer to survival level than teaching level, so Eden had offered to help with the class. Two hours a week for six weeks in the slower part of their catering year—March and early April—seemed like a decent way to give back to the community.

Lois had done all the groundwork, polling the men to find out what they wanted to learn, figuring out balanced menus with the help of a nutritionist, strong-arming a few of the guys into coming for their own health and well-being. All Eden had to do was instruct. Making food was empowering, and she enjoyed helping people move from intimidation to enthusiasm in the kitchen. She sensed that with this group, however, she might have her work cut out for her.

Several of the men appeared less than happy to be here, and Lois had told her that some had never fended for themselves before losing their wives. They ate whatever was handy, usually unhealthy fare. As for the younger two…Eden had no idea why they were there. Chaperones, perhaps?

"Shall we get started?" she asked as she walked over to the station where her demonstration was laid out.

Her remark was met by total silence. Finally a short, gnarled guy in a red plaid shirt growled, "What the hell. Why don't we?"

Hearing Lois inhale deeply behind her, Eden smiled to herself. This guy she liked.

"WE'RE GOING TO begin with eggs," Eden Tremont said. She was small and blond with cheerleader good looks. All the guys, even Gabe, seemed to be standing a little taller now that she'd started the class. "For some of you," she said, "this may be new, for others it's not, but practice never hurt anyone."

Nick glanced to his left and then gritted his teeth. Again.

What in the hell was Marcus doing here?

Studiously avoiding his eyes, that's what, which made Nick nervous. Marcus had somehow adopted Lenny, one of Gabe's closer friends and an ex-cop, and was working at the counter right next to Nick and Gabe.

Eden quickly demonstrated what she wanted the guys to do, then set them loose and started circulating, calling out instructions. Gabe stood staring at his bowl. Nick shifted his weight impatiently, but kept his mouth shut, having learned a long time ago how to handle his grandfather.

"She said whip the eggs until they have some air in them, kid," Lenny said to Marcus, whose hand was a blur as he beat his eggs with a fork, "not turn them into a foamy mess."

Gabe exhaled heavily and morosely broke an egg, reaching into the bowl with one of his thick fingers to try and get out a piece of eggshell. He cursed under his breath.

"Gimme another egg," he said after wiping his hand on a paper towel. Nick handed him another from the carton they were sharing with Lenny and Marcus. As soon as he could get Marcus alone…

"Don't you want to join in?" Eden Tremont asked from behind him.

He turned. "I, uh, am just here with my grand-dad."

"You can still cook."

"I haven't paid for the food or anything."

"I'll bill you," Eden said. "I'm billing him." She jerked her head toward Marcus, who was now ahead of everyone else and pouring his eggs into a pan. They practically exploded on contact.

"Too hot," Eden said, stepping over to lower the heat under the pan. "Everyone, please make sure your burner is set on low heat."

"I thought you said you were here to learn to cook, so you wouldn't have a heart attack like I did," Gabe said.

"I can learn by watching."

Eden came back and set a clean skillet on the counter in front of Nick. "Use this pan. Cook some eggs. Make your grandfather happy."

Gabe gave a soft snort as he started stirring his

eggs in the bowl. A few minutes later, he said, "You know, she's cute."

"Yeah."

His grandfather tapped the spoon on the side of the bowl. "Aren't you ever going to start looking again?"

Nick sucked in a breath. It'd been over two years since he'd lost his wife in a car wreck. And no, he hadn't started looking again. "This isn't the time to discuss this, Granddad."

"When is?"

Nick shook his head and reached for an egg. He cracked it on the side of the counter and the whole thing blew up in his hand, splattering yolk on his shirt and pants.

"Good one," Marcus said.

Nick gave him a shut-up-or-you'll-be-wearing-an-egg look. The accountant took the hint and went back to his stirring.

"Thin-shelled egg," Eden Tremont said from behind Nick. "They need to feed the chickens more calcium."

"Good to know," he said, glancing down at the yolk spots on his pants. Eden smiled at him and he smiled back, wondering what it would take to get her to trust him.

"The cleanup towels are over there by the sink.

Just throw them into that container when you're done."

"Will do. Thanks."

"This is lame," Gabe said as he poured his eggs into the pan, but Nick noticed he was smiling a little. His grandfather had never been much of a cook.

"Maybe," Nick said, "but I learned some things about eggs." Such as milk wasn't good to use for scrambled eggs. Water was better.

Once they finished cooking, Eden talked about various kinds of bacon—beef, turkey, pork and a soy product she called bacon-oid. The guys got a kick out of that one, but when she offered them a taste they seemed to think it was a reasonable alternative for those who couldn't eat regular bacon due to the high-fat and sodium content.

Lois had nodded with happy satisfaction during the mini lecture. Indeed, the old guys seemed more prone to listening to a pretty and petite blonde than to a woman who looked as if she could wrestle them into submission if they didn't eat right.

While Eden was talking, Nick pretended to pay attention as he debated which of those closed door across the room might hold a computer and how he could get at it. There was a computer in the front reception area, but he doubted it was linked to financial accounts. He would check it out, though. When he got the chance. It probably wouldn't be during cooking lessons, due to the open layout of the place.

Every now and again he caught Marcus shooting small glances his way. Another problem.

Oh, yeah. He and Marcus were going to have a discussion, and soon, because Nick was damned afraid of what the accountant might be up to. Especially after assuring Daphne he was not a dweeb.

As soon as class ended and Lois started the guys toward the bus, Nick said goodbye to his grandfather and sprinted a few feet to intercept Marcus on the way to his car.

"Why are you here?"

His colleague adjusted his glasses and squared his shoulders. "I have my reasons."

"Why don't you share them with me?" Nick's worst nightmare was that Marcus was here on some kind of an I'll-show-you mission.

"I want to learn to cook."

"I'm going to count to three…." Nick said.

Marcus's eyes got wider behind the lenses of his glasses. "All right. I came here thinking that maybe I could ask Eden Tremont out to coffee or something. Get to know her."

This was his way of manning up? Proving he wasn't a dweeb? Nick could live with that—he just didn't know if Eden could.

"I thought I might be able to come up with a way to get at her computers personally, review the information, and save you the trouble of trying to hack in and download," the accountant added.

Nick's eyebrows rose. How had Marcus planned to do that? Maybe while Eden was in bed asleep, after an invigorating romp?

His mouth went flat. "I can see, though, that I'm not her type."

"Yeah?" Nick asked. "How can you see that?"

"Because she was ogling you."

Nick snorted. Ogling? Somehow he had missed that, and he didn't miss much. But it had been a while since his woman radar had been up. Two years this past January.

"Therefore," Marcus said smugly, "the obvious solution is for *you* to get to know her better. And I can help."

"Please don't help," Nick said instantly.

"Too late." He gave one of his superior smiles. "I've already laid the groundwork."

"What groundwork?" Nick growled.

Marcus simply smirked and then started for his car without giving an answer, leaving Nick staring after him.

Groundwork... He hadn't had time to lay any, whatever the hell he had in mind. Nick had been within a few feet of Marcus the entire night, and other than a couple quick conversations with Eden... The guy was delusional.

And a pain. "Hey!" Nick shouted. Marcus turned back. "How'd you hook up with Lenny?"

His colleague shrugged. "I stopped by Candlewood and asked the woman if I could put in some community service hours. Told her I worked for Reno PD, and showed her my credentials."

"Well...it worked."

"I know," Marcus said smugly, before turning back toward his car.

GABE STOOD NEXT to the van, between the vehicle and the sidewalk, not exactly eager to settle himself in one of the uncomfortable seats, and heartily wishing that Lois would hurry up already. But he could see her through the kitchen window, still talking to Eden Tremont, the cute teacher who'd been watching Nick all night. Just as Nick had been watching her.

Gabe felt a stirring of hope. As far as he knew, Nick hadn't shown any kind of interest in a woman since Miri, and he'd definitely been focused on the teacher tonight.

Gabe smiled a little as he recalled Nick telling him he wasn't taking the class because of the teacher. Ha. So much for that. This was a good beginning and Gabe was going to see to it that Nick and the teacher got some alone time.

But right now he was tired and wanted to go home.

He resisted the urge to knock on the window to hurry Lois along and instead started up the steps into the van. Once he got into the van and took his seat beside Lenny, he could see that Nick hadn't left yet. He was on the far side of the parking lot talking to that dark haired guy who'd attached himself to Lenny.

"So who was your little helper?" Gabe asked.

"Damned if I know," Lenny said, half turning in his seat. He reached up to stroke the edge of his mustache, as if he was a detective solving a case in an old movie. Drove Gabe crazy when he did that. "Marcus somebody. He just showed up and told Lois he wanted to help out."

"And adopted you."

"Guess he knew talent when he saw it."

Gabe snorted.

"You know what I think?" Lenny asked in his gravelly voice.

"No way of knowing," Gabe replied sharply.

One last stroke of the mustache. "I think he's hot on the teacher. Couldn't take his eyes offa her. Probably doing this to get to know her better." Lenny smiled. "Clever."

"Oh, give me a break," Gabe muttered. "That's not clever. It's so obvious that...well...it's just obvious."

"Nick was watching her, too."

Gabe sucked a short breath in between his teeth. He didn't want his grandson to be as obvious as that Marcus kid.

"You'd have to be blind not to watch her," Gabe said. "In case *you* didn't notice, she's an eyeful." And exactly what his Nick needed to ease back into life—a spunky, beautiful girl, who knew how to cook.

Even though he thought Nick had a much better shot at catching her eye than Marcus did, he was now feeling a whole lot better about setting things up so that the two of them had a chance to talk again—without eight other guys and hawkeyed Lois there to watch them.

"YOU WERE WONDERFUL with them," Lois said after the last guy had taken off his apron and headed out to the Candlewood van. As near as Eden could tell after two meetings, Lois didn't smile much, but she was smiling now. "I think this program could really take off."

Eden's eyes must have gone wide because Lois quickly added, "No, we won't take advantage of you. But this could be just what we need to talk the shareholders into building a decent-size cafeteria on the premises." She reached out and patted Eden on the shoulder. "I'll be in contact about next week's meal."

Eden went with her to the door, pausing at the window to watch Nick walking back toward his black SUV, while Marcus got into his sports car. Odd pair. Marcus had chatted her up while he'd cooked his second pan of eggs, explaining that he was an accounts analyst and that his friend Nick was in home security. Both of them worked long hours and this was a great opportunity to spend time with their elderly relatives.

It had been a lot of information crammed into a very short conversation.

And now Marcus didn't seem to be getting along too well with his friend. Obviously they'd had a discussion, and not a happy one from the look on Nick's face. He glanced up as he approached his vehicle, and his eyes met hers through the glass. There was a frozen moment of connection before he looked away and opened the car door, his expression taut. Businesslike.

Feeling oddly unsettled, she turned as he got in his SUV, and went to finish closing down the kitchen.

"IT's GOING TO be a surprise!" Tina Ballard said, leaning on the counter in the Tremont kitchen reception area, her gold bracelets rattling on the granite surface. Her younger son, Jed, stood behind her, jangling his car keys and generally looking bored as only a teenage kid could.

Eden jotted down the word *surprise* and drew a circle around it. Tina beamed. She was trim and tanned from playing tennis, her dark hair perfectly cut. "His birthday is on the fifteenth. It's a Tuesday, so that should really make it a surprise. Who has a party on a Tuesday?"

In addition to cooking for the Ballards every week, Eden had catered many of their parties, but never on a Tuesday. "Not many people do that," she agreed.

Jed rolled his eyes. The Ballard boys were just a touch spoiled. Their father worked as entertainment director of several hotels in the Cassandra chain, including the Tahoe Summit. He pulled in one heck of a salary, but he'd always been down-to-earth and personable. As was Tina.

"I'll work up some menus and be in contact," Eden said.

"Good." Her client patted the counter. "Oh, I heard that Justin finally got the Firebird going."

"Yes, he did," Eden said. And she hated it, because he drove too fast.

"Michael will be pleased. He only sold it to Justin because of you, you know."

Eden smiled. "I thought it was because of all that begging."

"That, too."

Jed gave a small cough and Tina straightened up from the counter. "We'd best be going. I know you'll do a spectacular job with this."

"I will," Eden agreed, as her best customer waved and disappeared out the door.

Good money, good times, but surprise parties were a pain.

She went back into the kitchen, where Patty

was running a basin of warm water to wash the counters down after a full day of making chicken potpies.

"I thought Justin would be in by now," Patty said.

"Double shift at the Tahoe Summit," Eden told her. Again.

"He does too much," Patty said. Eden didn't answer, since the prep cook said that at least four or five times a day, but she did glance at the clock. It was later than she'd thought.

"Oh, man, I've got to hurry. I told Reggie I'd be at their place at seven." It was her babysitting night, an evening she looked forward to, since she couldn't quite get enough of her new niece, Rosemary Eden Gerard. Tom, Reggie's husband, put in long hours renovating the house he was going to use as the site of his new restaurant, and he insisted that they get one night out a week.

"You know I don't mind finishing up here," Patty said briskly. "I like cleaning at the end of the day."

"Thanks." Eden didn't hesitate in accepting her offer. Patty did like cleaning up, finishing up, locking up. Being indispensable. And in a way, Eden felt sorry for her. Other than at Tremont, she didn't seem to be indispensable to anyone.

Eden hung up her apron, thanked Patty again, who waved her off, then rushed out the front door to the lot. And stopped dead when she saw the envelope stuck under her car's windshield wiper.

Drawing in a breath, she yanked out the heavy envelope. Cream colored and expensive—no doubt who had left it there.

Eden dropped the envelope on the ground and got into her car. She'd pick it up and throw it away some other time. But right now, even though she couldn't see his car parked anywhere, she had a strong suspicion that Ian was watching, waiting to see her reaction to whatever he'd written.

He wouldn't be getting a reaction from her because she wasn't going to allow him to engage her. She jammed the key into the ignition and started the engine, letting it run for a few seconds before she put it into gear and backed out of the parking spot.

She noted with a touch of satisfaction that she'd run straight over the envelope, leaving a nice dirty tire mark on the pristine cream paper.

"IT's OPEN," TOM GERARD called when Eden knocked on the back door of her sister's house. Brioche, her brother-in-law's part-Yorkie dog, raced across the kitchen to greet Eden, nearly sliding out the door as she skidded to a stop on the tile floor.

"Hey, Bree," Eden said, leaning down to ruffle the hair of the little terrier's head. The dog grinned at her and danced on its hind feet. Mims, Reggie's fat cat, watched disdainfully from the kitchen door, but Eden knew that before the evening was over, cat and dog would be snuggled together in one bed.

"Thanks for coming," Tom said, handing Eden the baby and then gently prying tiny fingers off his slate-blue silk tie. Rosemary's lower lip jutted out as she lost possession of her new find, so Tom made a silly blowing noise at her stomach. The baby gave a huge gummy grin and waved both hands. Tom laughed.

"New trick," he said to Eden with a crooked smile. "There's a bottle in the fridge ready to go. Just heat and serve in about an hour, and she should go down."

Not if Eden had anything to do with it. The baby might go to sleep, but she'd be in Aunt Eden's arms in the rocker while they overdosed on classic movies.

"I need to hurry my wife along so that we can eat and be back before Reggie falls asleep."

"I swear she's pregnant again," Eden said.

"Not likely." But he didn't look displeased by the idea. "And she's not throwing up."

"It's probably a boy. Different chemistry involved."

Reggie came out then, her dark hair swept up. She was wearing an emerald-green dress that made her look cool and elegant, exactly the opposite of how Eden felt nine-tenths of the time. Somehow blond and short did not translate into cool and elegant. She might have felt on the edge of sophisticated at Reggie's wedding, and maybe at one or two of her proms—not the one where she fell in the fountain, thanks to her brother—but in general she had to settle for being the perky Tremont.

Perky.

She hated that word.

"You look great," Eden said, transferring the baby to her shoulder, in case Reggie had any ideas about relieving her of her burden.

"Thanks." Reggie came around behind her to kiss the top of her daughter's head. "We won't be long. I got the payroll done. Don't let me forget to give you the checks."

"They're on the dining-room table," Tom said, helping his wife into her coat.

"How're things at the kitchen?" Reggie asked as Tom firmly shepherded her to the door.

"All caught up." Barely. Eden patted the baby's back. "You know we'll call you guys if we get into the juice, and in the meantime you can stop worrying, stay home and enjoy motherhood."

Which was exactly what Reggie was doing. She'd promised to take six months off, coming back in May when the wedding season started gearing up, and to everyone's surprise she'd kept her word.

The baby hiccupped and Eden wondered what the back of her sweatshirt looked like. Cute as they were, babies seemed to make a full-time career out of emitting fluids.

"You're fine," Reggie said, reading her mind. "See you—" Her words turned into a laugh as Tom propelled her out the door.

"Later," he finished before firmly closing it.

"Just you and me and the menagerie, kid," Eden said as she crossed the room to the rocker recliner, with the dog and cat trailing close behind. Brioche curled up with her chin on Eden's shoes and Mims jumped onto the nearby sofa to keep an eye on things.

For a few minutes Eden simply sat and rocked the baby. It had been a long day. All her days were long, so that wasn't anything new, but ending it with an unread and unwanted note from Ian was.

Crap.

She should have read it. Maybe she'd stop by on her way home and pick it up from the parking lot, see what he had to say.

Or maybe she should just leave matters alone. She was better off not knowing what he'd written. Then it wouldn't weigh on her mind. She wouldn't have to think of how to handle matters.

But she wouldn't be prepared, either. And perhaps it was simply a goodbye. If so, she wanted to know that she could stop worrying about him pestering her to give him a second chance.

Okay…she'd stop and get the note. Even though it was going to ruin her night.

Eden rubbed Rosemary's back, drawing in the wonderful fresh baby scent as she cuddled her niece close. Hard to think about anything bad in the world when holding a soft, warm baby. Since it was probably going to be a number of years before she had one of her own, Eden shoved all the rotten Ian-related thoughts out of her mind and focused on what was in the here and now.

ROSEMARY WAS ASLEEP in Eden's arms when Reggie and Tom returned home at nine o'clock, and Reggie did indeed look as if she was ready to conk out. Eden gave Tom an I-told-you-so look before she passed the baby to him. He winked at her and in turn handed the baby to Reggie, who barely managed to say, "Thanks so much for sitting," before she yawned.

"Same time next week?" Eden asked as Reggie came back out from the baby's room. Her sister glanced at Tom, who nodded.

"We may not be going out for a while."

Because you're pregnant and nauseous?

"Lowell has asked me to help with his restaurant for a month. It'll pay off a big chunk of the renovation bill for my place."

Ah, yes. Lowell, Tom's best friend in the culinary world. Eden had never quite known what to make of the brash Scot, but he had a solid reputation as a chef and restaurateur. "So…you're going to France?"

"For four weeks…while Lowell deals with some personal issues."

"Is his wife divorcing him again?" Eden asked.

Tom simply shook his head and Eden decided not to ask for details.

"As soon as we get back, I'm coming to work at Tremont," Reggie said. "Part time. But this seems a good way to finish up my time off."

"When do you leave?" Eden would miss her sister. And the baby. But this was a spectacular opportunity. Especially for Tom, who was still trying to reestablish himself in the cooking world after a few missteps the previous year.

"A week and a half."

"Short notice," Eden commented.

"Lowell is kind of that way," her brother-in-law stated.

Eden had met his giant friend, a mercurial bear of a man, and had to agree. Lowell was impulsive.

Tom put his arm around Reggie's shoulders. "Once I open my restaurant, it'll be damned hard to get away."

"You don't have to explain to me," Eden said. "I agree that it's a great opportunity." Her mouth quirked up at one corner. "But could you maybe leave Rosemary here with me?"

The couple looked at one another and then back at her.

Reggie simply shook her head. "Uh…no."

Eden left the house smiling, happy for her sister and brother-in-law. The dog and cat would stay with Tom's former neighbors, Frank and Bernie, who would be able to give them tons more attention than Eden or Justin.

Life was going well for Reggie, and was the usual blur for Justin. As for her...well, she had an ex who was showing signs of getting out of control, and she was going to do something about it.

THE ENVELOPE WAS gone. Eden had fully expected to find it right where she'd run over it. What were the chances that some passerby had seen it and picked it up, perhaps hoping there was money inside?

Or had Ian come back and retrieved it, tire mark and all? That hypothesis was rather satisfying.

Of course now Eden wanted to read it more than anything. After searching the bushes, in case a gust of wind had blown it out of the lot, she got into her car and headed for her house, two miles away.

Eden pulled into her driveway and parked. Her house was so small that the garage was the only storage space she had, so that was where Christmas was stored, as well as her seasonal clothing and all the hobbies she'd started and meant to take up again, but hadn't because she didn't have the time. Plus, she had all Justin's sports gear in there. Definitely no room for a car.

She pulled the keys out of the ignition and

was about to get out when the motion-sensor light at the side of the house came on, startling her. Two neighborhood cats, the sensor culprits, came strolling out to the front, their eyes reflecting greenish-yellow as they stopped to stare at her. Her house seemed to be located on some neighborhood migration path. The light came on at least once or twice every evening, and within two weeks of moving into the place, Eden had stopped looking out the window to see what had triggered it, because it was always the same— cats.

Although, she thought on her way to her front door, this was a classic horror-story setup. Complacent heroine, evil marauding terror. Zombies, perhaps. She fitted the key into the door and turned it. Maybe she should just take a quick peek out the window every now and then to see who or what was passing by.

Or maybe she should stop letting the envelope get to her.

But what if Ian hadn't put it there?

CHAPTER THREE

"THERE ARE three computers," Nick said. "Two in the back office and the other in the entry area before you go into the kitchen. There's a file cabinet in the office—"

"Oh, shit." Daphne let her head fall forward, her forehead hitting the bar with an audible thunk that made the whiskey in Nick's glass bounce. "He's here," she said without moving. "I should never have told him to man up. Now he's hellbent on proving to me that he is."

No doubt whom she meant.

Nick understood why Marcus had a thing for Daphne. A lot of the guys did. She had a killer body, long black, wavy hair and a damn fine face. Plus, she could outshoot most guys in the department. But she wasn't going to hook up with Marcus, and it would be a hell of a lot easier on everyone in the immediate vicinity if he'd accept this.

"Hey." Marcus pulled up a stool on the other

side of Daphne. "Are you feeling all right?" he asked, as she raised her head and pushed the hair back from her face impatiently.

"I was."

"Why are you here?" Nick inquired, before Daphne could skewer the guy.

"I saw your truck outside." Marcus raised his hand to get the bartender's attention. "Corona, please. With a lime."

"Are you sure you don't want one of those sixty-four-calorie light beers?" Daphne asked politely.

"What does that mean?" Marcus looked down at his flat stomach, as if wondering if she was suggesting he was fat. Not fat. Just a wiener, but Nick hoped she didn't tell him that. Not when they needed his assistance—although he did seem totally impervious to insult.

"We were kind of having a private conversation," Nick said.

"Oh. Well I didn't mean to butt in." Marcus's voice was clipped. "I just thought we were kind of a team."

"We are a team," Nick said wearily. They needed him, as annoying as he was. "So why don't you tell me about this groundwork you've laid."

Daphne took a drink of her beer and a few drops fell onto the front of her blouse. As she brushed them away, Marcus's eyes followed the movement like a tracking beam.

"What groundwork?" he asked, glancing away from her chest.

"You said at the cooking lesson that you'd laid groundwork," Nick reminded him.

"I *hope* to lay some groundwork," Marcus corrected.

That wasn't what he'd said, but Nick wasn't going to argue fine points. He laid a palm on the bar and leaned closer to the accountant. "I do not need help with the getting into Tremont Catering part. I need help with the files after I get them. *That* is your job."

Marcus smirked. "You aren't the only one who can indulge in covert operations."

Covert operations? Daphne frowned at Nick, who rolled his eyes skyward. It beat choking their teammate.

"Look," she said, turning her attention back to Marcus, "we all have our jobs. Yours is behind a desk, and that's fine. When I told you to man up, apparently you got the wrong idea."

"No, sister," Marcus said, pointing a finger at her. "*You've* got the wrong idea. About me."

"You're an accountant," Daphne said patiently. "Nothing wrong with that."

"Do *not* patronize me," Marcus snapped. He sucked in a long breath that made him look as if he were going to explode. But instead of launching into another verbal assault, he exhaled sharply and headed toward the door.

"Hey," the bartender called. "Want your beer?"

Marcus stopped and fumbled for his wallet.

"I'll get it," Nick said.

"You can just go to hell." Marcus flipped a five onto the bar and then jammed his wallet back into his rear pocket before walking out.

"He's off his rocker," Daphne said when the door shut behind him and the other patrons turned their attention back to their drinks.

"But he's part of the team," Nick said darkly, picking up his beer again. "And he'd better not screw up my investigation by going rogue."

GABE WAS COOKING eggs when Nick stopped by to see him on Sunday afternoon as usual.

"Want some?" he asked, holding up the pan. He had a towel tucked into the front of his baggy slacks as a makeshift apron, making him look very much as if he knew what he was doing.

"No," Nick said, noticing that there wasn't enough to share. "I just ate. You go ahead."

Gabe slipped the eggs onto a plate and sat at his small table, the towel still in place. Nick sat opposite him.

"So you got something out of the lessons," Nick said with a touch of I-told-you-so in his voice.

"Yeah and so did you."

"Meaning?"

Gabe snorted. "You can continue to deny it, but you were watching the teacher."

Nick's mouth tightened. He hadn't been looking at Eden for the reasons his grandfather seemed to think he was.

Besides, his granddad wasn't around him enough to know whether or not he was looking at women. He'd looked. A few times. But he hadn't felt ready to act.

"You don't need to feel shifty about it," Gabe said. "It's been two years since Miri passed away." During which time Nick had buried himself in his work.

"I don't feel shifty about it." Well, maybe he did, but not for the reasons Gabe thought.

His grandfather shoveled eggs into his mouth,

then reached for the salt. Nick put his hand on the shaker first. "Remember what Lois says."

"Screw Lois." But Gabe abandoned his attempt to raise his blood pressure. "Hey, they're planning the casino night. It's on the fifteenth."

"I'll mark it on my calendar." Nick had been to every one of the semiannual casino nights since Gabe had taken up residence in Candlewood. Family came and participated, and Nick was the only family Gabe had in town, since his son and wife, Nick's parents, now lived in Las Vegas.

Gabe smiled in a predatory way. He loved to gamble. "I'm going to clean up, you know. Buy a new recliner."

"You have enough money to buy a recliner now."

"But it's more fun to win the money gambling." He cut his eyes sideways. "Which brings me to another issue."

Nick raised his eyebrows. "An issue?"

"Yeah. My wallet disappeared. At the cooking lesson, I think."

Nick stared at the old man for a moment, trying to figure out what was going on in his head. "This isn't a ploy to get me talking to Eden Tremont, is it?"

"Hell, no. If you don't have the balls to talk to her without an excuse—"

Nick raised his hand, interrupting. "Sorry. It's just that…" *I don't believe you, you old coot.* "I'll see what I can do about your wallet. Did you have any cash in it?"

"A few bucks."

"Credit cards?"

"Keep 'em in the strongbox."

"ID?" His grandfather was no longer allowed to drive, and hated having an official ID card instead of a license.

"Strongbox."

"Then all you lost was a couple bucks."

"And the wallet, which I wouldn't mind getting back. You see, my grandson gave it to me as a present."

JUSTIN WAS ALREADY busy in the pastry room when Eden got to work the next morning. Patty would be late due to an appointment, so Eden started prepping for a brunch the following afternoon instead of making phone calls to purveyors and clients as usual. She got a good hour of work in before she finally abandoned her veggies and went back into the pastry area, where Justin was applying a base icing. "Hey, uh…"

He looked up. "What?"

"I found an envelope on my windshield last night when I left around six o'clock."

"Just an envelope?" her brother asked patiently. "Or was there something in it?"

"I don't know what was in it. I figured it was from Ian, and I dropped it on the ground, because I was really hoping he was watching me. Then curiosity got the better of me and I came back after babysitting Rosemary, and it was gone."

Justin shifted his weight, holding the spatula in his hand in a way that made Eden think he could defend himself with it. "Has Ian been bothering you?"

"Haven't seen him in over a week."

"If he does…"

Yeah. Right. She was going to have Justin deal with Ian for her. Mmm-hmm. "I'll let you know," she said. It wasn't as if her ex-boyfriend was dangerous. He was just hardheaded and hated to lose. He was determined to convince Eden the guest-bedroom grope had been a one-time thing, a fluke. Eden wasn't buying it and didn't like being lied to.

"I'm serious," Justin called after her as she left the pastry cave.

"I know. And thank you," she called back.

But she did feel better knowing she had someone who'd watch out for her.

She went back to work prepping the veggies when the buzzer on the front door rang. Wiping her hands on a towel, she walked into the reception area, stopping in the doorway when she saw who was there. One tall, broad-shouldered, dark haired cooking student.

"Nick?"

"Hi." He looked almost embarrassed as he said, "I was wondering…my granddad lost his wallet. I'm checking all the places he's been. Which aren't too many."

"Black elk skin?" Eden asked as she reached beneath the counter and pulled out the wallet Patty had found tucked in a drawer that morning.

He nodded. "That's the one."

"Your grandfather lost his wallet in a drawer."

Nick let out a long breath. "No doubt." He fixed her with sea-green eyes and said, "Just to give you a heads-up…I think my grandfather did this on purpose so that I would come down here and talk to you."

Eden laughed. "Enterprising."

His smile was slow and charming, although she didn't think he meant it to be.

"Are we the victims of geriatric matchmaking?" she asked, realizing that in spite of the Ian debacle, she didn't mind. In fact, Nick Duncan was kind of a nice distraction.

He cleared his throat. "I think so."

"What shall we do about that?" she asked innocently.

"Anything we can not to encourage him."

Eden took a moment to process his answer, and decided that he wasn't being insulting. No, he had nothing against her—he was trying to keep his grandfather in line. "Not in the dating market?"

"It's not that, it's just..."

"Hey," she said. "None of my business." Nick was interesting and she'd play this by ear. But there was something he could help her with. She tilted her head slightly and asked, "Would you mind giving me some security advice?"

The stunned look on his face made her wonder if she'd said something wrong. "You are in security, aren't you? Marcus told me you were."

"I didn't mean to look so surprised," he said as his expression cleared. "It's just that, well, I haven't been at this for too long."

"Have you been at it long enough to take a look at my back entrance and tell me what you think?"

"Sure," he said. "I take it you've been having some issues."

"Our prep cook found a man loitering near our van when she left the other night."

Eden led the way through the kitchen, past Patty, who was busily stirring away at the stove.

"Do you have an alarm system?"

"We never saw the need, since it's a kitchen and there's really nothing to steal."

"Are any of you ever here alone at night?"

"My brother. My sister and I tend to go home at a reasonable hour." She opened the door and said, "I thought you might just check the lighting and locks."

Nick ran his hand over the door frame, then opened it and went outside. Eden followed him into the alley, where he closed the door and once again inspected the frame and doorknob.

"You have a sturdy door and lock. Not easy to jimmy." He looked around the dead-end alley. The Tremont van was parked on the opposite side, and he pointed at it. "That offers a good hiding place, as do those narrow passages between the buildings."

"Should I park the van out front?"

"Just be aware it can be used for cover."

He took a few steps back, frowned up at the

light over the door and those on the other side of
the alley. "The lighting's not bad, but staying out
of the alley is probably the first line of defense.
Be aware of your surroundings. Keep away from
bushes and cars in the front lot, too. Don't come
and go after dark if you can help it."

He met her eyes, his expression quite serious.
"I wish I had a better answer."

"Me, too," Eden said, "but it'll have to do. The
city is changing."

"Well, people are trying to fight back. That's
why I do what I do."

"I guess so." She took a backward step. "I appreciate you taking the time to look at this."

"No problem. And Eden? If you have any more
trouble with guys hanging around behind your
building, let me know, okay?"

"You got an in with the cops?" she asked with
a smile.

"Yeah," he said seriously. "I do."

NICK WAS GOING to have to hurt Marcus. Security. This was obviously the groundwork he'd
laid. What was going on in that guy's squirrelly
brain? This was how he was going to maneuver
Nick into gaining Eden's trust? By having him
evaluate the locks and lighting?

Also, Nick hadn't planned on hiding his occupation as a cop, since he figured his reason for being there was legit enough not to raise the Tremonts' defenses. It wasn't as if he was asking questions about their finances. But now… it was going to look damned strange to have his "friend" Marcus saying one thing and him saying another. So he had another lie to cover.

He was going to have to find Marcus and discover the next step of the master plan so he could circumvent it.

If the accountant would even talk to him.

Maybe Nick should let Daphne shoot him, as she'd often threatened to, or maybe wing him. Just enough to put him out of action until Nick could get the information he needed.

EDEN WAS AT the computer working on menus for a new brochure, a bit ahead of schedule for a change, when the office door opened and Ian walked in. No flowers this time, but she felt like banging her head on the keyboard all the same. He was one of the best-looking men she'd ever dated. Twice. Tall, dark blond, muscular. He could get any number of women—probably women who wouldn't care if he cheated—but no. He had to keep after her.

"I want to talk," he said flatly. He adjusted the lapels of his wool blazer, telling Eden that he meant business. "And since you've been avoiding me, I came here."

"I've been avoiding you because we have nothing to talk about."

"You are absolutely wrong." He spoke as if it was the last time he was going to say it. Eden certainly hoped so. "We have several issues to clear up. Some things you need to understand."

"I saw you groping your friend's wife."

"Damn it, Eden. I was drunk. Frustrated. And *she* came on to *me*."

Eden put a hand to her head as he spit out the classic it-wasn't-my-fault argument. "Frustrated?" she demanded, mashing her hair down as she wondered how on earth he could possibly use *that* excuse. "I don't see that you had any reason to be frustrated. It wasn't like we didn't—" She abruptly shut her mouth and glared at him. Finally, she said through gritted teeth, "What kind of frustration?"

There was a very long moment of silence, then Ian said, "I need variety. It's the way I'm wired." He shoved his hands into his jacket pockets. "But it doesn't mean anything."

"Variety?" she repeated in a deadly voice.

Surely he didn't mean… "You need to see other women."

"You need to understand that I love you. *You* are the woman I want in the *forefront* of my life. To share the important aspects."

Eden had no idea what he was talking about. "The what?"

"Forefront. You are number one. The woman I want to have kids with."

She could barely believe what she was hearing. "I'm number *one*. But…" she sucked in a breath before saying darkly "…there are other numbers?"

"Not serious ones."

Eden clenched her fists. "Not serious?" Her voice rose sharply.

Ian's expression became impatient, bringing harsh lines to his handsome face. "Be realistic, Eden. It's normal to be attracted to other people while in love with only one."

"But you don't have to screw them. You have been screwing them, right?"

"It doesn't mean anything."

"Oh, please. Don't give me that bullshit."

"It's true."

"How many other times have you done this? Worked out your frustrations elsewhere? With those who are not number one? Did you do it when we were together before?"

He glanced sideways before looking down and then back up at her.

"You're kidding," Eden said flatly, unemotionally, although her stomach felt like a tight fist. "You've been screwing around on me and then have the audacity to tell me that I get the honored position of number one?"

"It wasn't serious," he repeated hotly.

"Then why didn't you tell me?"

"Because I suspected that you would react this way." He folded his arms over his chest.

"Oh, you mean you were afraid that I would take exception to being lied to and made to look like a fool."

"That wasn't my intention," he said, lifting his knuckles as if to caress her cheek, calm her.

Eden automatically jerked back. "I don't care what your intentions were," she said between her teeth. "I only care about the outcome."

His eyes shifted again, became thoughtfully assessing. "It's not that I cheated on you, is it? It's the fact that you felt foolish."

What an idiot. "Goodbye, Ian. Take your forefront position and offer it to some other woman. Or better yet, shove it up your ass."

He turned on his heel and stomped off. It wasn't until the door banged shut behind him that Eden realized she hadn't mentioned the envelope.

EDEN DROPPED BY Reggie's house on the way home from work that night to deliver a meal. She'd made extra for herself, but wasn't feeling all that hungry, and she didn't particularly look forward to going back to her lonely house. Besides, Reggie was leaving in a matter of days to join Tom in France, and Eden wanted to bounce a few things off her before she left.

"I thought you had a date," Reggie said when she answered the door. Rosemary, dressed in tiny denim overalls and a lacy pink shirt, was cradled in the crook of her arm.

"Nope. I have food," Eden said, walking into the spotless kitchen and setting the containers on the counter.

"When I stopped by to pick up the time sheets this afternoon, Patty told me you had a date after you made your deliveries."

"Not a date," Eden said, touching the baby's cheek and watching her smile. "Patty misunderstood. It was coffee with Jason." The former star quarterback from her cheerleading days was now the staid owner of a sporting goods store. "He called me today and wanted to talk about his divorce." Eden let out a sigh and met her sister's eyes. "I couldn't do it. I canceled."

After Ian, she didn't want to hear about *anyone's* relationship issues.

Reggie shifted the baby onto her hip. "You never cancel on Jason. You always let him pour his heart out to you."

"Ian came by today."

"Yeah?" Her sister went into instant protector-mode. "What did he have to say?"

"What he had to say was that I'm stupid for not allowing him to screw around."

"Excuse me?" Reggie said, affronted.

"Yes. I am to be the front woman. The one with the house and the kids, because he loves me, you see. The other women he screws…he doesn't love them, so it doesn't count."

"What a scumball."

"Perfect assessment," Eden said, reaching for the baby. "And I told him so."

"So it was more than the woman at the party?" Reggie popped the lids off the containers and put them in the microwave.

"I guess it was going on while we dated the first time around, as well."

Reggie's hand hovered near the keypad. "No

kidding." Her arm fell to her side. "Should I even bother with the food? Are you going to be able to eat?"

Rosemary cooed and squirmed, and Eden held her closer, breathing in her sweet baby scent. "Yes," she said adamantly. "And do you know why?"

"No."

"Because I'm not going to let some jerk like Ian disrupt my life. Eating is a pretty big part of my world."

Reggie pushed the button.

"You know what else?" Eden asked, rubbing her hand over the baby's back.

"Not a clue," Reggie said, getting two plates out of the cupboard and setting them on the table.

"I'm not going to let this jerk destroy my confidence."

"Good."

"I hope," Eden amended. The truth was, as good as it felt to utter those words, her confidence was severely rattled.

When the timer dinged, her sister put the warm containers filled with fettuccine Alfredo and scampi ala marinara on the table along with serving spoons.

"The thing is," Eden said as she filled her plate

with one hand, balancing the baby on her lap with the other, "I keep dating the *same* kind of guy. Hell, I keep dating the same guy. Charming. Professional. Upwardly mobile. Cheating. Scheming. Lying."

Reggie laughed, but there was a cautious edge to it.

"I need to keep an open mind. Consider all the many possibilities out there that are not Ian. Maybe I just need a wild rebound fling."

"Maybe," Reggie agreed.

Eden let out a sigh. "I guess what I really need is to remember that Ian is an asshole and that there are better men available."

"The best revenge is living well," Reggie quoted.

"Right now I'd settle for living adequately with people I can trust."

Reggie lifted her glass of water in salute. "Here, here."

The baby started fussing not long after Eden loaded the dishwasher, and Reggie started yawning, so Eden drove home feeling tons better after unloading to her sister.

Ian was simply an unpleasant blip on the radar. She wouldn't allow him to be anything more.

The motion sensor light was on when she

drove into her driveway, telling her that a cat must be in the vicinity. Or so she thought until she walked into the house and shut her front door. It slammed shut easily, whereas she usually had to give it a little push.

A chill chased up her spine.

Her front door closed easily only when the back door was open.

CHAPTER FOUR

EDEN TOOK A backward step, then turned and yanked the door open. She shot outside, running down the sidewalk to her car as if she was being chased—which she was, for all she knew. Blood pounded in her ears, so there was no way she could have heard a pursuer.

Thank goodness it was impossible to get her car into the garage.

She climbed inside, locked it, and only then did she chance a look at her house, half expecting someone to be staring back at her out the open front door.

Nothing. Just blackness. And both her neighbors' houses were equally black.

The motion-sensor light clicked off automatically, making Eden jump in her seat. She sucked in a breath and dialed 911.

She was going to look kind of stupid if the back door wasn't open, but she wasn't checking it herself, and there was no way she was phoning Justin. He'd have to do the manly thing and investigate on his own. Someone could still be in the house, and she wasn't going to risk her brother when she could have a trained professional handle the job.

Twenty-five minutes later a police cruiser pulled up and Eden got out of her car. She was still nervous, but nearly half an hour spent sitting on her quiet street watching her house had made her wonder if perhaps she'd jumped to a wrong conclusion. Perhaps the back door wasn't open....

It wasn't.

But someone had thrown a large rock through her bedroom window, creating the same effect. Eden didn't know whether to feel vindicated or horrified. Both, perhaps. She wrapped her arms around herself as she talked to the police officer in the spare bedroom, where the big rock lay beneath the window, glass shards scattered around it.

"No one you know who'd have a reason to do this?"

"I, uh…"

"Any bad partings with friends or boyfriends? Neighborhood feuds?"

"I recently broke up with a guy, but this isn't his style." Although, honestly? Risky back bedroom shenanigans hadn't seemed to be his style, either.

"Name?"

"Ian Bartelli."

"Address?"

Eden gave his street and office addresses, then shifted uncomfortably. Her gut was shouting that this wasn't Ian's modus operandi...but maybe running over the envelope and then telling him what a jerk he was today had sent him over the edge.

"Are you going to talk to him?"

The officer drew in a breath that made his shoulders rise beneath his uniform, then closed his notebook. "Unless there's a witness—" and he'd already checked with the neighbors and satisfied himself that there wasn't "—we don't have the manpower to run down leads on a vandalism case. I can't make any promises."

So that's what she was. A vandalism case. "What if it was an attempted robbery?"

"With no witnesses, we really don't have anything to go on."

Eden pressed her lips together as she focused on the officer's shoes. Shoes very much like those Nick Duncan wore. "I understand."

"Do you have anyone you can stay with until you get this window fixed?"

"My sister."

The officer started walking down the hall to the kitchen and Eden followed, wondering if she would ever feel safe in her home again. "Have there been other occurrences of vandalism in the area?" she asked, a little ashamed of how hopeful she sounded.

"We have a lot of this kind of stuff." The officer spoke with both honesty and concern, which she appreciated. "You might want to invest in some better locks for your doors and windows."

"Won't do much good if they break the window, will it?"

"'Fraid not. A big dog might, though."

"I'll give that some thought." Eden didn't want to admit that she was kind of afraid of big dogs. Brioche, Reggie and Tom's little dog, was about as much canine as she could handle.

The officer was kind enough to wait the few minutes it took her to pack a change of clothes and her small jewelry box, which contained the only things she couldn't replace if they were stolen, and then walk her to her car. She thanked him, then got in her vehicle and waited for the cruiser to disappear around the corner before she flipped an illegal U and drove in the opposite direction, hoping that everything would be still in her house when she got back.

When she was three blocks away from Reggie's she called to ask if she could have a bed for the night. The answer would, of course, be yes, but Eden hated worrying her sister, so she'd waited as long as possible to phone.

Reggie didn't answer the first time Eden phoned, so she tried again. This time her sister picked up on the second ring. "I was sleeping. Sorry."

"No. I'm sorry," Eden said. Sorry she was adding worry into her sister's life. "I'm almost at your house, and I need a bed for the night. Okay?"

"What's wrong." It was a statement, not a question.

"Just…I'll tell you when I get there."

"How far away are you?"

"Pulling into the drive."

Reggie had the back door open by the time Eden turned off her car. She locked the doors and walked up to Reggie and Brioche, who were waiting for her. Instead of moving aside so Eden could come in, Reggie stood in the doorway.

"What happened?" she asked.

"Someone threw a rock through my back window. The police have been there and we agreed that I should sleep somewhere else tonight."

Her mouth had fallen open almost as soon as Eden started her explanation, and now she snapped it shut. "Of course you shouldn't sleep there. And you didn't call Justin, did you?"

"I'm not stupid," Eden muttered as Reggie shut and locked the door, then turned the dead bolt. Eden set the jewelry box on the counter where she'd put the food containers earlier that evening, and dropped the plastic grocery bag with her extra clothing on a chair. For a moment they stood staring at each other across a few feet of tile, then Eden rubbed her cold hands together. "The police officer thinks it was just a random thing."

"Not Ian?"

"Come on, Reggie." Eden reached down and scooped up Brioche, who was still dancing at her feet. She cuddled the little dog close. "Is this the kind of thing Ian would do?"

"We didn't think he'd do what he did with Vanessa, either."

"Touché," Eden said wearily, having already had that argument with herself. She stroked Brioche's ears. Random act of vandalism. Scary, but unlikely to happen again...that was really easy to believe in her sister's warm kitchen. How easy would it be to believe tomorrow, in her own house?

"Are the cops going to talk to him?"

"Maybe, maybe not. He said they're short on manpower."

Reggie took Eden by the arm and led her into the living room, where she maneuvered her onto the sofa and took a seat next to her. "You should stay here while we're in France. I'll feel better."

"Actually, I might just get a big dog. That's what the cop suggested."

"You're afraid of big dogs."

"Well, only Fluffy, really. She kind of traumatized me. When you reach out to pet a dog named Fluffy, you don't expect to be bitten."

But she had been—fortunately, not badly enough to have to go to the emergency room. That was Justin's thing. He was on a first-name basis with a couple of the doctors there. It'd been hell chasing their father down and getting a verbal for treatment when they were growing up. Finally, he'd started leaving a permission-to-treat note with Reggie and the problem had been solved.

"You could borrow Brioche while we're gone."

Eden's shoulders slumped as reality set in. "I won't be home enough to care for a dog. I'll have to come up with something else. Like an alarm system or neighborhood watch."

When Reggie reached out and hugged her, Eden let out a long shuddering breath and clung for a moment before easing away. She wasn't a kid anymore. She was a woman who needed a bed for the night, and then she'd reevaluate the situation in the light of day.

And she might be a woman who needed to consult a security expert.

NICK BROUGHT GABE'S wallet back on laundry day—or rather laundry night. Three or four times a month, Nick showed up after work and helped Gabe haul his laundry to the coin washers in the basement. There was a laundry service for a cost, but so far Gabe had refused. It gave him a good excuse to spend an evening with Nick, who occasionally brought his own laundry.

"You found it," Gabe said after Nick pulled the wallet out of his jacket pocket and set it on the table.

"Yeah," Nick said, fixing him with the dead-eye. "Aren't you going to ask where?"

Gabe cleared his throat and reminded himself which one of them was the respected elder. "Where?" Acting had never been his forte, so he usually relied on grumpiness to get him through dicey situations.

"Apparently it was in a drawer."

Gabe forced his forehead to wrinkle in surprise. "A drawer? How in the hell…? I put it on the counter. Lenny or someone must have…"

Nick's mouth tightened briefly, telling Gabe that he wasn't buying the Lenny defense.

"Or I may have put it there. Just to get it out of the way. I'm old. My memory…"

"Bull," was all Nick said, and then he walked over to the laundry duffels Gabe had packed that afternoon, and hefted one in each hand.

They left the apartment and walked to the service elevator in silence. Down they went, and after the door slid open directly into the laundry facility, Nick led the way to the nearest washer and lifted the lid.

And still he didn't say anything.

"What's eating you?" Gabe asked. Was Nick ticked because of the wallet? If so then he needed to come right out and say it. But he didn't, so Gabe decided to help him along. Clear the air.

"Let me put it this way," he said. "What's bugging you? Grandfather, woman or job?"

He was hoping for woman, but suspected grandfather.

"It's a case."

Job. Hmm. "Drugs?" Of course it was drugs, since Nick was on that task force. But he was trying to initiate a conversation.

"Missing C.I., actually."

Different kettle of fish, that. Gabe gave a small shrug. "Those guys go to ground all the time."

Nick started dumping the bag of dark clothes into the washer while Gabe did the same with the light. His movements were slower than Nick's, but he got the job done. "Not this one. He…it's hard to explain. He was enough of a criminal that guys in the trade trusted him, but—" Nick shook his head, as if he couldn't believe what he was about to say "—he wanted more out of the job than money."

"What could he have gotten out of snitching?"

"He wanted to become an undercover cop." Nick glanced over at Gabe then. "He was saving his money to go to POST training to become a real cop. It wouldn't have happened, of course. Not with his background, but the kid had a goal. And he was likeable."

"You sure he wasn't playing you?" Confidential informants got their money and then often spent it on drugs—perpetuating the very thing that the police were trying to take down with the information the C.I.s sold them.

"Yeah." Nick poured in some soap. "He was slick, but had this odd kind of sincerity about him. I liked him, and I don't usually warm up to those guys." Gabe took the box of soap from him. "He disappeared just before a big meeting that was going to help us break a case. Daphne isn't taking it well."

"Daphne doesn't take anything well." For a brief period of time, Gabe had tried to encourage Nick to see Daphne as something other than a partner, hoping to get his grandson out of his funk, but after a few hours in her company, he decided that Daphne was too much of a scary pain in the ass to have as a granddaughter-in-law. Or even to momentarily distract Nick.

Besides, it would have ruined a decent professional partnership. She and Nick worked well together.

"No. I mean she's kind of broken up about it." Nick fished change out of his pocket to feed the machine and dumped it on top of the washing machine.

"Ten to one the kid got scared and skipped." Gabe reached out to take a few quarters.

"Damn, I hope so." Nick actually sounded like he was kind of broken up about it, too.

"Must be a special kid," Gabe muttered, even though he still didn't believe for one moment that a snitch could be anyone special. He'd yet to meet one that wasn't more than willing to play the ends against the middle whenever and wherever possible.

"Yeah," Nick said.

"Let me know how this all works out," Gabe said as they started back to the elevator to go upstairs and watch TV while the clothes washed.

"Sure thing, and in return, I have one favor to ask of you."

"What's that?"

"Next time we go somewhere, leave your wallet in the strong box. Okay?"

PATTY KNEW SOMETHING was up, but Eden hadn't told her what had happened, thinking that at least one of them should be focused on the job at hand and not wondering if the window had yet to be replaced in her house, and how she was going to find the nerve to sleep there tonight. Reggie had offered her the spare room for as long as she needed, and Eden was thinking about taking her up on it for at least another couple nights.

"Lovely luncheon," Patty said with deep satisfaction after the last guest had left and they began gathering linens, counting napkins, packing leftover food into coolers. "And I'll have dinner tonight." Eden always let Patty take home any unserved portions. "I was wondering…could I take home enough of this lasagna for two?" She spoke without looking at Eden.

"Sure." There was only enough left for two. "Company tonight?" To Eden's amazement, Patty blushed. "A date?"

"No, no, no," she assured her. "Just company."

All the same, company meant that Patty currently had a fuller social life than Eden did.

"Certainly. Take the lasagna. There's a couple extra crème brûlées, too. Just bring the dishes back." As if Patty wouldn't.

"Oh, that's not necessary…." She smiled, but to herself, not at Eden. "All right. Thank you."

Interesting, Eden thought as she dragged a cooler to the van, where Justin had just packed the display boxes.

"You know I'm going over to your place before I start work tonight," he said.

"I didn't know you had to work," Eden answered in an undertone.

"Not at the Lake. Just a quick birthday cake."

"How quick?"

"Sheet cake. A few roses. Some lettering."

"Why don't they go to a bakery?"

"Hey," Justin said with mock disgust. "Because I do it better…and charge a lot more. We all know that the more you spend, the better the quality."

"Well, that works, because I have my cooking lesson tonight. You can escort me home afterward and then go back to your baking."

"Oh, yeah. The geezers."

"Do you mean the elderly gentlemen?"

"That is exactly what I mean," Justin said, smiling for the first time since he'd heard about the rock.

Once back at the kitchen they unpacked the van, and then, with less persuasion than usual, Patty allowed herself to be sent home with her containers of food. Justin did a quick inventory of the fridge contents and realized he was out of mint and raspberries for his umpteenth eleventh-hour cake.

"Do you need anything?" he asked as he headed out to Whole Foods.

"Nope. Lois is bringing the ingredients and the students." Most of them, anyway. Eden wondered if Nick and Marcus were going to show up to chaperone their grandfathers again. "All I have to do is teach them how to make chili."

"Good luck with that," Justin said.

"It's fun. You'll be surprised."

"No, I won't," he said. "Because I'm not coming out of my lair while they're here."

JUSTIN TREMONT'S BLUE Firebird was parked in front of the catering kitchen when Nick arrived for the class. He gave the sports car a quick once-over as he locked his vehicle, admiring the lines.

Purchased with drug money? Or financed to the hilt?

If all went well, he'd soon have the answer to that question.

Snooping around in financial records was not sanctioned in any way, shape or form, but getting a records search warrant was nigh impossible when the only tie was that Tremont worked for a hotel that had drug traffic, and he was part owner in a small business.

Small businesses were an excellent way to launder dirty money and, to Nick's way of thinking, reason enough to look at the records. The judge he'd talked to informally disagreed. He told Nick it was not only a stretch, it was a huge stretch. There was no law against working a job and having a business.

Lois was helping Lenny out of the van when Nick walked around the rear end to where his grandfather was waiting.

"Did you see that car?" Gabe asked.

"Hard to miss, since I parked next to it," Nick replied.

"I always wanted one of those."

Well, if a Firebird came up in a police seizure auction, Nick would buy it for him—even if he couldn't drive it legally. "Why didn't you get one?"

"The women in my life said no. Said I'd drive too fast."

"Would you?"

Gabe snorted in response as Lois led the way to the door. She tried to hold it open, but Lenny took over for her.

Nick's gaze went to Eden the instant he walked into the kitchen, even though he'd told himself that he was going to ignore her as much as possible during the lesson so as not to encourage Gabe. There was simply something about her that drew the eye. And made it hold.

She smiled at the group in general as they traipsed in, and Nick could almost hear the old guys give a collective sigh, but something about her smile seemed more forced than last week.

Maybe teaching old guys was harder than she'd thought it would be. Maybe she hadn't expected to be the subject of an impromptu geriatric matchmaking scheme.

Eden had just stepped up to the area where she gave her opening talk when the door opened again and Marcus came in. He quickly made his way to the far side of the group—far away from Nick, who smiled to himself. Grimly. He was going to find out exactly what Marcus was up to, and put a stop to it.

"Today we're making chili," Eden said, and everyone perked up.

Paul raised his hand. "What about heartburn?"

"We're keeping the spice low and the fat lower. The fat is more of an enemy than spice. You guys do not have to give up tasty food because of heartburn."

Lois held up her hands as all eyes turned her way. "I'll inform the cook," she said.

Nick knew that many of these men fended for themselves, using canned food because the cafeteria "slop" was so bland.

"First of all," Eden continued, "you have to get a decent cut of meat. Nothing less than ground sirloin, which is low in fat. If your budget is tight, use less meat and more beans...."

Eden was smiling as she spoke, doing a decent job of captivating the older guys, but Nick couldn't shake the feeling that something was off.

During the last lesson, she'd exuded personality. Tonight she seemed tense, almost walled off. But she kept smiling. And his grandfather and cronies kept smiling back as she extolled the virtue of prechopped onion and garlic, and the differences in canned tomatoes—crushed, diced and whole.

Lois had brought all the ingredients, which were divided into individual plastic containers that two people would share. Gabe pulled the lid off their container and started unloading ground sirloin, onions, garlic, tomatoes. The very stuff Eden had talked about. Nick got the ground meat out and opened the package.

"She said to cook the onion first," Gabe snapped, taking out the plastic bag of chopped onion. "Weren't you listening?"

"I'm just opening it."

"Why aren't *we* cutting the onion?" Gabe muttered as he set the bag on the counter and then went to the stove he was sharing with Paul and Hal. Tremont had two large stoves and there was room for two teams of two at each. Nick was glad that Marcus and Lenny were at the other stove.

"Ask Eden or Lois," Nick suggested, eyeing the doors on the other side of the room. Faint music came out of one—Justin Tremont working, maybe? The other door was open and a computer was clearly visible. Nick wouldn't be doing much during lessons with his target in such clear view. Now it became a matter of how to get back into the building after the lesson was over and Justin gone.

Nick looked back at the stove in time to see Gabe pour about half a gallon of oil into the pan to fry the onions. "Oops," his grandfather said.

"Gabe…" Lois came out of nowhere, shaking her head. "She said two tablespoons. That's two cups."

Gabe gave a small, unrepentant snort.

"Uh, yeah." Nick reached for the handle and sloppily poured oil back in the bottle, glad the pan wasn't hot. Otherwise they would have had to deep-fry their onions.

The pan went back on the stove, and once the oil was heated, Gabe dumped the premeasured onions in and started stirring while Eden called directions from the other stove, where she was demonstrating with Lenny's pan. Marcus was studying her, but not the way he studied Daphne.

Lois stayed at Gabe and Nick's stove, overseeing the browning process, while Eden stayed at the other. Nick kept an eye on her, wondering if the computer in the reception area was networked to the one in the office. That computer he could get to.

"When the meat is done, we'll stir in the tomatoes," Eden called.

"Hey," Nick said to Gabe. "I need to get something out of my car. Be right back."

"What?"

"My phone," he said.

"What is it with you guys and your phones? Can't you live for two hours without it?" Gabe held up the premeasured bag of chili powder. "There's not much here," he said to Lois in an accusing tone.

"It's strong," the woman said drily.

Nick left the kitchen for the dimly lit reception area. He could hear Justin's music through the wall as he approached the computer. It was turned off. Eden had her hands full, but he wasn't going to turn it on. He'd come back as soon as he figured out a way in.

He'd just turned away to head to the door, when Eden joined him. "Why aren't you cooking?" she asked.

"I forgot my cell and I'm expecting a call."

"I see. I'm here for the same reason." She walked over to the computer desk and pulled open a drawer to retrieve a phone. He was damned glad he hadn't touched the thing. "Company phone. I leave it with my brother when I go home for the night."

"Does he get a lot of business calls after hours?" Nick asked dubiously.

"No. He turns his own cell off so he can concentrate. If my sister or I have an emergency and need him, then we can call this phone. That way he doesn't have to stop what he's doing and screen calls." She came to stand next to Nick in the doorway.

"Clever."

She smiled, and again he had the strong feeling that she was putting up a front. She was so different from the last time he'd seen her. "Is everything all right?"

She flashed a startled look up at him. "Excuse me?"

"You just seem…subdued."

She glanced away from him and over to the

men, who were completing their assigned tasks in the kitchen with a bit more enthusiasm than during the first lesson. More confidence, perhaps. Lois moved from group to group, encouraging. When Eden looked back at Nick, she said, "Actually, I was going to ask for a bit of advice before you left."

"Security advice?" What had Marcus done now?

Her mouth flattened into a straight line. "Someone threw a rock through my window the day before yesterday."

Nick pulled his hands out of his pockets and barely refrained from saying, "No shit?" Instead he asked, "Do you know who did it?"

Eden shook her head. "I think it might be time for a security system. In fact, my sister will give me no peace until I get one. Could you offer any suggestions?"

It took Nick a moment to answer. Of course he'd give her suggestions. Just as soon as he looked up some information on the security systems available. Finally he settled on, "I'd be happy to. Maybe we could set up a time?" Before she could answer, he added, "I won't try to sell you anything."

Her forehead wrinkled. "Why not?"

That's it. Put your foot in it, Nick. "What I meant is, no hard sell. I'll give you information on what's out there. If you decide to go with someone else, I'm good with that. The important thing is to get you into a more secure environment." He shut his mouth before he rambled anymore, or worse yet, put his foot in it again.

"I appreciate that." She smiled at him with such sincerity that Nick felt a twinge of guilt. "Maybe Saturday morning?"

He pretended to consider his schedule. "Yeah. That works. I'll meet you at your house and take a look?"

"Great. My brother will undoubtedly be there, too."

"Do you live together?"

"No," she said drily. "I live with his toys. He has a condo. But he's my technical advisor."

"Great." This made it a hell of a lot easier to figure out if Eden had anything in her house worth looking at—like, say, a computer. And what kind of toys Justin stored there.

The only thing that bothered Nick was that this was way too easy. Almost as if someone had planned it.

CHAPTER FIVE

"GETTING MIGHTY cozy with the teacher," Gabe said as Nick walked with him to the van after they finished their cleanup. Nick carried a cardboard box with six large plastic containers of chili for the guys to take home.

"Stop now," he said. Gabe waited while Lenny climbed up into the van. "And by the way, she doesn't know I'm a detective."

"She got something against cops?"

"Not that I know of. I just want to keep my head down, and, well, she thinks I'm in security."

"Working on a case?"

"I'll explain later. Okay?"

"Gotcha." Gabe obviously wanted to ask questions, but didn't.

Nick smiled. "Hey, lessons aren't so bad."

The old man shrugged. "I get to spend some time with you."

The reply startled him. "Didn't we spend time before?"

"Yeah, but it was kind of boring. You sitting there in my apartment, probably counting the minutes until you could leave."

"I was not counting the minutes. You're the one who didn't want to do anything."

"Because you don't golf."

"You don't go to baseball games."

"Well, now we both cook. You can come over once a week and help me whip up some grub."

Nick laughed and so did Gabe, but it turned into a cough. "Are you okay?" Nick asked, patting his back.

"Fine. Fine. I'd better get into the jitney before Lois has a fit. See you next week if not sooner." Gabe raised a hand and then got on the bus and took a seat next to Lenny.

Nick waved to his grandfather. As he lowered his hand he caught sight of Marcus skirting the parking lot toward his car, looking very much like a crab scuttling for cover. The bus pulled away and Nick jogged across the small lot to intercept him. After talking to Eden he had a theory as to why Marcus had had nothing to say to him during lessons.

"Did you throw a rock through Eden Tremont's window?"

Marcus's expression, which was first stunned

and then instantly defensive, more than answered the question.

"You asshole," Nick said. "That's vandalism, you know. Who the hell's going to pay for that window?"

"I didn't throw a rock." He brushed his dark hair off his forehead with a jerky movement.

"Yeah. Just like you didn't want to show Daphne that you could be a procedure-flaunting badass."

Marcus tipped his chin up defiantly. "If I *had* thrown a rock, it would have been to get *you* access to Eden Tremont's home and business." One corner of his mouth twitched. "Which you now apparently have."

"How do you know?"

"I heard her talking to her brother while Lenny and I were cleaning up." Nick opened his mouth, but Marcus spoke before he could. "You can now get access to her computers."

"And you'll analyze it." *Even though I called you an asshole.*

"Daphne may not take me seriously, but I do have skills, and I will use them to help you guys find out what happened to Cully."

"It may not help your case with Daphne," Nick said honestly.

"And then again," Marcus said, "it may. I'll take my chances."

Marcus got into his car and slammed the door, leaving Nick staring at his profile through the side window.

"'GETTING MIGHTY COZY with the teacher?'" Lenny mimicked when Gabe took his usual seat beside him. Gabe felt color creep up his neck and into his face.

"That was a private conversation." He hadn't realized that Lenny's hearing was better than most of the other guys'. "And he's getting a lot cozier than your helper is."

"Yeah," Lenny conceded. "I no longer have a horse in this race."

"I can't believe you ever thought you did," Gabe said on a snort.

Lenny leaned toward him as the van started to move and said, "But I don't know that you do, either—not if you keep pushing your grandson that way. You gotta be more subtle. People hate to be shoved into things."

"I'm not shoving him," Gabe snapped. "And there's a lot more to this than you know." Maybe he had pushed slightly tonight, but he was getting impatient. It didn't have to be this woman, but he'd like to have some sign that Nick wasn't going to spend the rest of his life buried in the job before he, Gabe, croaked. Just an inkling that Nick wasn't following in Gabe's ignorant footsteps, because he'd made some huge adjustments that were still haunting him. Ignoring his wife until she left him was one. Not marrying the woman he should have ten years later was another.

He didn't want Nick to reach his age and wish that he'd done something beside chase bad guys.

"It looks like you're shoving from where I'm standing."

Gabe turned in his seat. "You want to see some shoving—"

"Stop now," Lois said coolly, making eye contact in the rearview mirror as she drove.

Gabe held his breath, waiting for her to say something that would make him feel like a schoolkid, but she didn't, which in turn meant that he wouldn't have to set the record straight as to who was paying whom for services. Her gaze dropped back to the road.

Gabe leaned closer to Lenny, who was now staring straight ahead and muttered, "I am not shoving and even if I were, it's none of your business."

ON FRIDAY MORNING Nick cruised down Eden's street in his pickup truck—an older model diesel he'd bought from his grandfather after his heart attack. The engine made a hell of a racket, so much so that he couldn't go through the drive-through window at a fast-food joint without turning the engine off in order to be heard—perhaps not the best vehicle he could use to unobtrusively case the neighborhood, but he enjoyed driving it. He only needed to nail down what he'd be dealing with so he could do a buttload of Google searches and collect the proper brochures from the various home security companies he planned on visiting that day. Good thing he was suspended, he thought with grim humor, or he wouldn't have time to do all this research.

Eden lived in an older part of town, where the majority of houses were one- or two-story brick, with mature landscapes that provided good cover for anyone looking to break in. But in spite of that, the neighborhood was relatively crime free. According to tax records, there were few rentals, so the population was stable. The meth heads hadn't moved in. All in all, it wasn't a place where residents needed to take huge security precautions. Still, robberies, break-ins and assaults could happen anywhere.

A hedge-lined alley ran between Eden's property and the house next door, which would have made it very easy for Marcus to toss the rock through the window.

The lighting on the alley side of the house was ridiculously inadequate. An antique motion sensor was tacked to the siding and there were no pole lights. In this day and age there was no excuse for poor lighting.

A wildflower garden dominated the front yard, which was a hell of lot better than shrubbery, but the honeysuckle bushes next to the garage had grown up past the windows. Another concern to be addressed.

He turned the corner at the end of the block and headed toward Virginia Street, even though he wouldn't have minded making another pass by the house. The truck was just too noisy for that.

In twenty days he'd be back on the job, and a whole hell of a lot more vigilant about what he said and did, because he did not want to spend another month sitting on his hands. And before those twenty days were up, he wanted a solid lead that he could take to the lieutenant, or even the captain, about the drug traffic at the Summit and Cully's disappearance.

EDEN WAS UP at dawn Saturday morning, her one day free this week. She'd seen Reggie and Rosemary off the night before and had a strong feeling that her sister wouldn't have left if Eden hadn't had this security appointment in the works. But she did, and she planned to kill the five hours until Nick showed up doing laundry.

And she would have, if the washing machine had chosen to cooperate.

After the second load, the annoying tiny leak in the cold-water hose had become a full-fledged flood—more than duct tape could handle—and she'd had no choice but to turn off the water at the source and drive to the hardware store to purchase a new hose.

She'd just finished swapping out the hoses when the doorbell rang. Exactly ten o'clock, the time Nick was due to arrive.

Okay. Points for promptness. Unfortunately, the way the morning was going, Eden would have given more points if he'd been late, or blown off the entire appointment. She wiped her hands down the sides of her jeans as she walked from the kitchen to the living room, and then automatically looked out the peephole before opening the door.

Instant blood pressure spike. Ian, not Nick, stood on the other side.

Eden took a step back, her heart pounding a little harder. It might just be another push to get her to listen to him, but after everything that had happened, she wasn't taking any chances.

"Answer the door, Eden!"

Oh, yeah. That was a tone that made her want to open it. Especially after the rock and the envelope. "Go away or I'm calling the cops," she said, loudly enough to be heard through the door.

"You already did that, didn't you?"

Eden pressed a hand against her forehead. Damn. The officer had said he probably wouldn't have a chance to talk to Ian, but apparently he'd come up with some free time.

"I didn't throw a freaking *rock* through your window and you had no right to tell the cops it was me!" Ian shouted.

"I didn't tell them it was you. I told them I'd just broken up with my cheating boyfriend."

"And gave them my name."

"They asked for it."

There was no answer. For a long moment Eden stood staring at the door, wondering if she dare open it. Justin was held up in construction on the

Pyramid Highway, but Nick should be here any moment.

"I'm expecting company," Eden said shortly.

"Good for you."

"I wasn't trying to cause trouble, Ian. I was just trying to find out who threw a rock through my window." And she still wasn't certain it wasn't him.

"Well, you did cause me trouble, because the bloody cop came to my office. My boss is asking questions."

Eden pulled the door open, shifting her weight as she locked eyes with Ian, one hand still on the door, blocking his entrance. Oh, he was angry. His jaw was set, his perfectly cut dark blond hair ruffled, as if he hadn't bothered to comb it that morning.

"Tell him we did not part on the best of terms after I caught you and Vanessa going at it, so I irrationally accused you of a crime you didn't commit." She paused for a moment, studying him. "That's what you did tell him, didn't you?"

"Pretty much."

"So why are you here now?"

"So that you understand that if it happens again, I'm pursuing harassment charges."

"Pursue away, Ian," she said, as a truck with a

loud diesel engine turned onto her street a block away. It chugged to a stop in front of her house, behind Ian's Audi.

"My company is here," she said when Nick turned off the ignition and opened his door. Ian's gaze automatically followed hers, and then his lips curled disdainfully.

"Nice truck. What's his name? Billy Bob?"

"Goodbye, Ian."

"Remember what I said."

"Burned into my memory."

Ian turned and stalked to his car, not sparing Nick, who had climbed out of his truck, so much as a glance.

Nick waited until he got into his car, then appeared to jot down Ian's license plate number on a small notepad as the lawyer gunned the engine and pulled out onto the street. Even at a distance, Eden could see Nick smirk before he turned and started toward her.

"Trouble?" he asked when he reached the porch.

"Ex-boyfriend," Eden said shortly.

"Rock thrower?"

"Not according to him."

"Do you believe him?"

"Right now I don't know what to believe,"

Eden said as she watched Ian turn onto a side street several blocks down, his tires squealing as he rounded the corner. Ian rarely showed anger, but today he had, and he was taking it out on his car. "I guess my objective at this point is to keep it from happening again. The rock, I mean."

"Your brother not here?" Nick asked.

She turned her attention back to him, debating whether or not to thank him for cutting Ian's caustic visit short, then decided against it. She hadn't needed rescuing, but if she had, Nick looked like the guy for the job. He wasn't gigantic, but tall and sturdy, with broad shoulders and a confident yet vaguely impatient air about him, as if he'd put up with only so much before he sprang into action and took care of a situation.

"Held up by road construction near the Nugget, but he should arrive anytime now."

"I can wait in my truck until he gets here."

Eden stepped back, holding the door open. "Come on in." Right now she felt a whole lot better about Nick than she did about Ian. "I have some coffee on, if you want a cup while I finish mopping up."

"Sure," Nick said, walking past her into the living room, then pausing to take stock as she closed the door. "Cleaning day?" he asked, noting the piles of damp towels in the hallway.

"Washer explosion day."

He frowned at her and Eden noted again how extraordinary his eyes were. They gave her the feeling that there was so much more going on in his head than he let on.

"A leak in my cold-water laundry hose suddenly got bigger. I was in the middle of fixing it when Ian got here."

"You fixed your own washer?" He seemed surprised. Eden didn't know why.

"It's only a hose," she said with a shrug.

Nick followed her into the kitchen, stopping in the doorway. "You have a nice place."

"Yes. I just redid this room." And she loved it. It had taken time, since she replaced things as she could afford to—pale cream granite countertops almost two years ago, the oak island after the huge Wilmington wedding last summer and the natural slate tile floor this spring. She'd painted the walls pale green and the woodwork white during her limited free time, and had tiled the backsplash herself.

"I like it," he said.

Eden walked around the island to the coffee-pot plugged in next to the fridge. She needed to put some space between them—not because he made her nervous, but because he made her feel aware. Just…aware. In a way she couldn't put her finger on.

"Have a seat," she said, a bit embarrassed that her voice sounded a little husky. Making small talk was part of her profession, but right now conversational tidbits weren't exactly jumping into her brain. Thankfully, he was wearing a gray University of Nevada Reno sweatshirt over worn jeans and a navy blue Wolf Pack ball cap. "Do you follow the Pack?" she asked as she poured him a cup of coffee.

"I do. How about you?" He took the chair she pointed at.

"Not too much," Eden said. She'd gone to culinary school, not the local university.

"Not a sports fan?" he asked, putting the brochures he was carrying on the table in front of him.

"I don't mind the occasional baseball game, but I haven't been to one since the Silver Socks disbanded."

"That's been a while." The semipro team had disbanded over a decade ago, and it was only recently that Reno had managed to get a new team, the Aces.

"I'm thinking I may get some tickets and see how the new team compares to the old." Eden set two cups of coffee on the table, on opposite sides, and took her seat. Nick pulled the cup toward him and lifted it to his lips. After sipping, he gave his head a small shake.

"Too strong?" Eden asked.

"Not even close," he said, his eyes meeting hers. "You should see the stuff I drink—"

Five rapid knocks interrupted him and then the front door opened. Nick shot her a questioning look, as if asking if he needed to shift into protection mode.

"Justin," Eden said.

"Your door isn't locked?"

"He has a key. He's just warning me it's him."

"Hey," her brother called from the other room.

"In here," Eden replied as he walked into the kitchen. For the first time in weeks, he didn't look as if he was going to pass out from exhaustion, and he wasn't dressed in his usual off-hours uniform of worn jeans and a T-shirt that had seen better days. Instead, he wore new jeans with a web belt and an oxford shirt, tucked in. And his hair was combed. He looked both respectable and somewhat commanding, despite the fact that Nick was at least four inches taller than him and fifteen pounds heavier.

"Nick, this is my brother, Justin. Justin, Nick Duncan."

Nick got to his feet and extended a hand. "Nice to meet you."

"Likewise."

Nick sat back down and Justin went to the cupboard, where he took out an oversize cup, then filled it with coffee.

"So, where are we?" he asked, pulling up a chair to the table between Eden and Nick.

"I was about to tell your sister that she lives in a relatively safe neighborhood, but that she needs to update a few things."

"How so?" Justin asked in a way that told Eden he'd been doing a bit of independent research.

"Better lighting and possibly an alarm system. I want to take a look around, and then I can give you a more in-depth analysis."

"I like the idea of an alarm system," Eden said. Then maybe she'd start sleeping through the night again.

Justin studied Nick. "Do you prefer a wired or wireless system?"

There was a brief silence before Nick said, "Depends on the house. In this case, I'd suggest wireless so we don't have to tear into the old plaster."

"But those can be triggered by any radio signal, right? A passing police car or anything?"

"It doesn't happen that often, and the wired systems have their share of problems, too. But either one would beat having no security at all."

"Agreed," Justin said, his tone giving Eden an instant bad feeling. "Do you work out of your home?" he asked Nick.

"Yeah. I do. Why?"

"Because I couldn't find a business listed in the Yellow Pages under your name."

"I'm just starting out." There was another short pause before he said, "Up until a few weeks ago I was a cop."

Before Eden could respond, Justin asked, "Laid off?"

"Personality conflict with my lieutenant," Nick said. "If you have a problem with my credentials—"

Justin shook his head. "You have to understand my position here. The only way we know you is through two cooking lessons. This is my sister."

Who can run her own interference.

"Just how much security do I need?" Eden interrupted, having had quite enough of the face-off. When she'd asked Justin to come for the inspection, she'd simply wanted another person with her, not a brother in overprotective mode.

"Let me take a look at the place and then we can talk." Nick met her eyes. "If you're still okay with it."

"Where do you want to start?" Eden asked.

"Doors and windows, followed by garage."

When he stood, she managed to catch Justin's eye, telling him quite clearly, with a simple raising of her eyebrows, to back off. He gave an unrepentant shrug. As always. Reggie had been the guardian of the family in all matters relating to money, health and school. Justin had fancied himself the muscle. And, for being a pretty normal-size guy, he was actually good at taking care of business. Eden didn't think he'd do too well with Nick, though.

"Wow," was all Nick said when he opened the kitchen door that led to the garage. Plastic storage bins were stacked along three walls and the rest of the garage was filled with loose stuff.

"I tend to start hobbies," she muttered. And to buy clothing and holiday decorations. A giant inflatable jack-o'-lantern, now just a flaccid length of black-and-orange nylon hanging from a hook next to the door, attested to that. "And

I also store things for other people," she said, giving her brother a meaningful glance. Justin lived in a condo on the Truckee River with minimal storage, so she was the keeper of the water skis during the winter, the snowboard and snow skis during the summer, the outboard motor, the kayak.

"At least I sold the Fiat," he said, referring to the car that had sat in her driveway for over a year, behind the Firebird, which had also been up on blocks, forcing her to park on the street.

"Finally." He'd always meant to restore the bucket of bolts, but between all his jobs, guess what? No time.

Nick wove a path through the cluttered garage to the window on the far side. The bushes outside had grown so high that it barely let in light.

"You need to prune back the shrubbery," he said. "Bushes make good hiding spots."

Eden nodded when he glanced back at her. She'd known that, but had somehow never thought she'd need to take such precautions in her neighborhood.

"I'll take care of that," Justin said.

"Seems like the least you can do, since this is also your storage area."

Justin looked as if he wanted to say something back, but didn't. Frankly, Eden was ready for the consultation to be over. She appreciated her brother coming to her place on one of his few mornings off, and she understood his suspicions, but the testosterone was getting a bit thick.

They went out to the yard and Nick inspected the exterior doors and windows, pointed out the places where she needed lighting, shook his head at her motion sensor. Finally, they went back into the kitchen, where Justin poured himself another half cup of coffee. He held up the pot, but the others shook their heads.

"So what do you think?" Eden asked Nick.

"You need new locks all the way round. An alarm system on the doors and windows would give you some peace of mind, but you could live without it if you fortify. You definitely need better lighting and you have to replace those antique motion sensors on your house."

"They work."

"You said that the neighborhood cats set them off," he explained patiently. "Newer models are not sensitive to small animals."

"How about bears?" Justin asked.

Nick gave no sign of reaction. "Bears would set off a sensor, which might be a problem at

Tahoe. But the last I heard, there weren't any bears in the general Reno vicinity."

"Just curious," Justin said.

"I'm not worried about bears," Eden interjected. "Just people. And I think I want some kind of alarm on the doors and windows."

"That'd give you more of a sense of security."

That was all she was looking for.

"How much?"

Nick met her eyes and she felt that same tiny zap of connection they'd had the first time he'd come to the catering kitchen. "I'll make some calls, see what kind of price I can get on a decent system. Sometimes I can get a deal on last year's models. I'll try to have an estimate worked up by Monday afternoon."

"How long will it take you to install?"

Nick shot Justin a quick look. "I'm not sure. Depends on the system. I'll have a better idea on Monday."

CHAPTER SIX

NICK WALKED TO his truck, wondering how he could manage a cram course in the fine art of security system installation before next weekend. He had no doubt that he could get the job done; he just didn't know if he could look like a professional while doing it. Obviously, he wouldn't be able to spend massive amounts of time studying the directions if Eden was there watching him, and he wouldn't be able to access her computer records, either. Solution? Make sure neither she nor her brother was at the house.

Nick might not find anything on her computer, but he was of the no-stone-unturned school of investigation. Sometimes clues to illegal operations showed up in unexpected places, and if Justin was involved, there was a strong possibility that his sisters—who did the books—were involved, too. In fact, they'd almost have to be. Which bothered Nick.

His big worry at the moment, however, besides

becoming an installation expert, was that one of the Tremonts would call Reno PD to check his story and find out he hadn't quit, but was suspended. But he'd had to tell a semblance of the truth. Flat-out lying about his occupation could have come back to bite him in the ass. The only thing he could hope for now was that the Tremonts had no reason to believe that he was insinuating himself into their lives for any reason other than cooking and security.

"What's your read?" Eden asked after the distinctive noise of Nick's diesel truck faded into the distance.

Justin grabbed his cup and took a swallow. "He sounded knowledgeable enough."

"Unlike some of us," Eden said as she opened the dishwasher and put Nick's mug inside. "'What do you prefer? Wired or wireless?'" she mimicked, closing the door.

Her brother grinned. "Hey, I didn't have much time to bone up." He swallowed the last of his lukewarm coffee.

"Obviously," Eden agreed. "But I was asking what your read was on getting a security system. Worth the money? Or will bigger and better locks and improved lighting do the same thing?"

"According to my research…" Justin began pompously, and then smiled. "You definitely need the locks and the lighting, which apparently this guy can do for you. A security system will probably make you feel safer while you're home—as long as you remember to turn it on."

"So it comes down to how much I want to spend to feel safe at night."

"I vote for the system," Justin said. "It'd make me feel better."

"Speaking of which…" Eden turned and leaned back against the sink, studying him with a slight frown. "Are you all right?"

"Why?" Justin said, sending her a cautious look.

"You appear well-rested."

One corner of his mouth curved up. "Appearances can be deceiving," he said drily, getting up and walking to the coffee carafe. He held it high as the very last few drops drained out.

"How long are you going to be able to keep this up?" Eden asked.

He didn't answer immediately; Eden knew he hated it when she pulled the big-sister act. Tough. It was no more annoying than the protective-brother bit, which *she'd* learned to live with, thank you very much.

"I'm young." A few seconds ticked by, and then he said, "I'll keep filling in for Maurie, the injured chef, until he's back on his feet. It's only one extra day a week. By the time I start making serious cakes," he continued, referring to the six orders he already had for May and June weddings, "he'll be back in the kitchen and I can go down to three days a week. And Patty's doing a great job with the desserts when I'm not there."

"You're burning a lot of gas driving back and forth, because I know you're driving the Firebird and not the Focus."

He smiled self-consciously. "I have to make time."

"And that worries me."

"Don't," he said, suddenly serious. "I'm fine." He drank the remaining coffee in a couple swallows, then went to rinse his cup in the sink. Eden stepped aside to give him access. "I'm going to take a few more hours off," he said, "then head over to the kitchen. What are your plans today?"

"The same," she said. They didn't have another event until midweek, so she wanted to do some office work. "No last-minute anything?"

"Not even a cupcake."

"Good, then maybe you can do a quick inventory of your baking supplies."

"Will do. See you in a few hours."

He started for the door, stopping to look over his shoulder. "This guy is probably exactly who he says he is, but I still want to be here when he installs the system."

"Maybe you can help me catch up on my housework."

Justin mouthed her words back to her and she laughed.

"Go home. Get some sleep. I'll see you at the kitchen later this aft."

NICK PARKED IN front of the Tremont Catering kitchen and gathered the brochures he'd collected the day before. He'd learned a lot about security systems, and once Eden told him which one she preferred, he'd do his research on installation and operational requirements.

The front door was open, so he let himself in and followed the sound of rhythmic chopping into the kitchen. Eden stood with her back to him in a simple knee-length, blue knit dress, orange rubber clogs and an apron. Her knife barely stopped moving as she finished one carrot and reached for another. He cleared his throat and she gave a small jump, whirling around, her eyes wide. When she saw it was him, she put the palm of her free hand on her chest and let out a breath. The other held the knife.

"I didn't mean to startle you," he said, and she smiled self-consciously.

"I'm not usually this jumpy."

"Nothing wrong with being jumpy," he said, holding up the brochures. "I brought by some information on the various systems, with the costs noted on them. I made a list of pros and cons so you and your brother can go over them. If you need additional information, then we can get together again before I order."

"Thanks. You can just set them on the counter, so I don't forget them when I go home." She reached up to brush a few tendrils of hair away from her cheek with the back of the hand that held the knife. The rest of her hair was pulled up in a messy yet somehow sexy knot.

He indicated the piles of chopped vegetables in front of her with a movement of his chin. "What are you making?"

"Mirepoix."

Nick moved his jaw sideways. "Which is?"

"Not as fancy as it sounds," she said with a smile that made him want to smile back. "Chopped-up veggies that go into a stock. I've roasted bones and now I'm going to simmer them in a liquid with chopped onions, carrots and garlic. Later, when Justin gets in, it should be done, and he'll strain it and put it in the cooler."

"How long does it simmer?"

"Five hours."

"Your brother comes to work at ten o'clock?" Good to know.

"He keeps nutty hours," Eden said with a disapproving quirk of her pretty mouth.

"But you keep normal hours," Nick said, although he really wanted to know about Justin's.

"I don't work at Lake Tahoe. Justin does."

"That's quite a drive. His job there makes it worthwhile?"

"He makes desserts at one of the bigger hotels there several days a week. It's a place where he can indulge his talent and get paid well for it."

"He's a pastry chef?"

Eden laughed. "Doesn't look like one, does he?"

Nick gave a slight snort. "No. So what does he do when he gets here so late?"

Eden walked over to a stainless-steel counter and Nick followed. "He bakes. It works, because a lot of what he makes can be refrigerated until we need it."

Nick needed to get out of there before Eden

got the idea that he was overly interested in the Tremont family business.

He was about to say, "Give me a call after you look over the brochures," when she leaned back against the counter, wiping her hands on a small towel. "Lois seems to think there may be issues using a chef's knife in this week's lesson. That some of the guys might not have the strength in their wrists and hands to use one correctly." She folded the towel and then looked up at him. "Would Gabe have trouble holding a knife the right way?"

"I don't think so." His grandfather seemed quite competent with all manner of weaponry. But Nick had to add, "I didn't even know there was a correct way to hold a knife. Don't you just grab the handle?"

Eden looked up at the ceiling in a way that answered his question.

"Wait here." She crossed the kitchen and reached into a bin at the far side, pulling out two large brown onions the size of baseballs. When she returned, she put them on the counter, side by side, then slid a cutting board in front of her before taking a largish knife off a magnetic holder. "Show me how you hold a knife."

Nick grasped the handle, extended his forefinger along the top of the carbon blade and prepared to chop, slice and dice.

"No."

He cocked an eyebrow. "How so?"

She put her hand over his, making his nerves jump at the contact with her warm palm as she moved his finger to one side of the blade and his thumb to the other, so he was pinching the steel while his palm rested on the wooden handle. It felt surprisingly natural. He'd never thought about holding a knife that way.

"Use the tip for small cuts, the back part for larger, and I think you probably know how to slice."

"Oh, I'm a slicing maniac."

"Okay. Slice that onion."

He picked it up and held it in his palm. "Peel it first?" She simply nodded, and he peeled the damn thing, feeling ridiculously awkward, as if his fingers were too big. He'd always hated peeling onions, and never used them unless he was making fried onions to go on top of his steak. Once he was done peeling, he placed the onion on the cutting board and began to slice. Nice thick, even slices.

"All right," Eden said. "Now, do you know how to dice?"

"I believe the first step is to plug in the food processor," he said sagely.

She snorted. "No. Let me show you." She demonstrated how to dice the onion by resting the tip of the knife on the cutting board and moving the handle up and down in a quick motion.

She diced half the onion, then said, "Now it's your turn."

Nick's movements were decidedly more awkward, maybe because his eyes were stinging from the onion and he could barely see, but he ended up with a pile of pieces. Some chunks were pretty big.

"Now a carrot." She pulled one out of the bag still sitting on the counter, and held it up.

"Are you game?" They were standing close enough that her shoulder kept touching his arm. And he liked it more than he wanted to. She was small and delicate, yet exuded energy. Plus, she smelled good. Like some kind of spice.

"So very game," he deadpanned.

There was no special trick to holding a peeler, but Eden showed him how to rest the tip of the carrot on the cutting board and turn it as he peeled. The economy of motion pleased him.

"When you cut anything, keep your fingers curled back and your thumb out of the way. Otherwise your hands will look like mine." She held up her finger to show him a crisscrossed scar. "Once wasn't enough for me. Took me two times to learn."

"Right," he said, with a lift of his eyebrows. "Curled back." He tried it out and Eden nodded. She showed him her slicing technique next, starting slowly, then increasing in speed until the carrot was whacked into incredible even slices in little more than a blink of an eye.

Shit. He'd hate to meet her in a dark alley with a knife.

"I guess I can see how you got those scars."

"Yes. I was in school, actually. A lot of blood flows in culinary school."

"I'd never thought about that."

"Fact of life," she said, once again brushing stray hairs off her forehead with the back of her wrist. "Now the celery."

Nick had never in his life thought he'd be embarrassed about the way he cut vegetables, but he wasn't exactly proud of the clumsily chopped celery he presented to Eden to toss into the pot of liquid. "Kind of amateurish," he said.

"It doesn't matter," she replied dismissively. "It'll get strained out. It's just a good way to practice cutting evenly for when it does matter."

"When is that?"

"Soups, stews, any number of dishes where the vegetables are eaten instead of strained out of the stock." She looked around at the counter. "I'm done. Thanks for the help."

He smiled. Maybe for the first time since he'd gotten there. "Yes. I was a big help. Thanks for the lesson. And give me a call once you and Justin have gone over the brochures."

After he got to his SUV, he paused for a moment before starting the engine. What was going on here? Eden was coming on to him—gently—but damned if he wasn't getting into it.

Two years of celibacy, and wasn't it just his luck that the first woman he'd felt a lick of interest in was a subject in an investigation?

CHAPTER SEVEN

"You gave him a lesson here alone?" Patty asked in a shocked voice.

"I checked him out with Reno PD," Eden said, more irritated than she wanted to be by Patty's attitude.

"You did?"

"Yes. He worked there until recently and is no longer active." Almost the exact words she'd been told.

Patty gave a humph as she digested that bit of information.

"Well," she said with a sniff, "I still think you should have someone with you in the building."

"You're right," Eden said. But she was going to do as she damned well pleased.

She sat down at her desk and started writing thank-you notes for the previous week's events. Later she would enclose evaluation sheets with folded self-addressed envelopes. After that she had to call the Ballards and get the final okay on the birthday menu, call a wedding planner concerning a possible menu substitution, and then she was free to go home. Early. Curl up with a cup of hot tea and read about alarm systems.

Her mouth tilted grimly. Lovely way to spend her first free evening in weeks.

DAPHNE WAS HELL on the shooting range, and when Nick shot with her, she invariably showed him up—as she was doing today. A lot of the guys in the department were intimidated by her, though they'd rather take a bullet in the leg than admit it. She didn't bother Nick, though. She reminded him of his mother.

After range practice, Daphne offered to buy coffee so they could talk without Marcus happening upon them. She'd once said that she thought he'd put a tracking device on her purse, because no matter where she tried to eat lunch, he'd show up. Frankly, after the rock incident, Nick wouldn't have been surprised.

They both ordered large coffees, black, and Daphne paid, since it was her turn.

"How's your grandpa?" she asked as she waited for her change.

"He's fine."

Daphne tossed the coins into the tip jar, then

led the way to an isolated table. "Do you think the lessons will work out?"

"I think they'll give me an opportunity to get into their offices, and thanks to Marcus and the rock, I'll also have access to her house." Nick took a sip of coffee and grimaced.

"That was a brilliant move on his part," Daphne said musingly, holding her coffee just below her mouth as she waited for it to cool slightly.

"He's doing it to impress you."

"It's working," Daphne said, taking a drink of the bitter brew without flinching. "I'm impressed that he was such a jerk. But I draw the line at letting him have his way with me."

"If you'd just tell him that, it'd save us both a lot of grief."

Daphne set down her cup. "Short of carving it into my forehead, what do you want me to do?"

"Carve it into *his* forehead?"

She laughed. "Do not tempt me."

"Speaking of carving, did you know there's a special way to hold a chef's knife?" Nick took a second taste of the coffee. It'd definitely been on the burner too long. Worse even than the stuff at the precinct.

"I didn't even know there was a designated

chef's knife." Daphne cooked about as often as Nick did.

"It's the long triangular one. Eden taught me how to use it today.

"How'd you do?"

"Not so good."

"Ah." His partner readjusted the lid on her coffee, which had leaked down the seam. "Anything else, beyond you sucking? Like any signs of conspicuous consumption?"

"They have a lot of fancy stainless-steel equipment and at least one stove is new, but I don't know if it all belongs to Tremont or to Tyler Corp, which owns the building. The catering van is brand-new. Tremont," he said, meaning Justin, "has a very nice Firebird. Classic. Eden said that they won some kind of a culinary contest last year and that business really picked up after that."

"How about Eden's house?"

He gave a small shrug. "No great shakes." But a hell of a lot nicer than his place. "Lots of clothes, and she stores her brother's toys for him."

"What kind of toys?"

"Skis, kayak. That kind of stuff. Normal guy stuff. There's nothing that shouts out conspicuous consumption." Which meant jack. "When I install the security system, I should be able to get a better feel for things."

"Good luck with that system," Daphne said before taking a big swallow of coffee. The woman was impervious to acid.

"Piece of cake," Nick said.

"Your next lesson is tomorrow?"

"Yeah. And I'm going to see if I can get to the computer while she's busy with the old guys." The download would take time, but he'd see what he could swing. "Last week they kept her hopping the entire time, so I may get lucky. The old guys are supposed to use knives, and she may have her hands full." He smiled slightly. "You should see her use a knife. It's kind of impressive."

"You might want to keep that in mind in case you end up arresting her," Daphne said.

EDEN ULTIMATELY CHOSE a security system that Nick could buy locally, and it was also one with a minimal amount of wiring. Two points in his favor. Now if he could just get the darn thing installed.

He'd bought a tool belt, which creaked because it was so new, making him very glad that he'd been up front about not being in the business for long. After going through the boxes, and figuring out what was what, he concluded that the system was the least of his worries. It was those damned sensor lights that concerned him.

Fortunately, there were many online videos that showed how to wire lights—a simple matter of disconnecting the old one and reconnecting the new using the existing wiring. It seemed a simple enough task, as long as there were no surprises. Surprises concerned him.

He'd also watched video clips on installing the locks and mounting the motion sensor lights. Again, not that complicated, and he could always bring the videos up on his phone if he needed a quick refresher. Thankfully, Eden had to work that day, so she wouldn't have the thrill of watching him try to figure out how to chisel out the wood for a dead bolt. That would also make it a whole lot easier to hack into her computer and copy her files.

Thanks to a few lessons from Marcus several months ago, and a special startup disk, Nick was competent in that particular area. He just hoped she didn't have any encrypted files.

NICK ARRIVED AT her door exactly at eight o'clock. Eden liked promptness in a man. There were other things she liked about Nick, too. His devotion to his grandfather for one.

Gabe spent a lot of time growling and barking during cooking lessons, and Nick let it roll off his back. Eden probably watched the two of them more than she should, but Nick drew her eye. And since she wasn't letting that jerk Ian and his underhanded ways upset her life, or her faith in men, she was indulging herself.

Nick did border on eye candy. Tall and broad shouldered, with close-cropped dark hair. And those green eyes.

Yes. Indulgence was good.

She smiled up at him as she opened the door. "How are you this morning?"

He raised the box he held in front of him. "Ready to make your home as safe as it can be."

"And how long will that take?" she said as she stepped back so he could carry it inside.

"I'm not certain." He set down the box and rubbed the side of his face. "With rewiring the lights and putting on the locks…hours?"

Eden almost asked if she was paying him enough. The price they'd settled on seemed low. But he'd set it, so she was going with it.

"How's your grandfather?" she asked as she gathered her purse and sweater.

"I believe the word is *irascible*."

"I like him." Eden put an arm into the sweater and Nick automatically reached out and held the garment for her as she slipped her other arm inside. "Thank you," she said, before adding, "We talked a bit at the last lesson while you were out at your car."

Nick rolled his eyes. "I'm certain he charmed your socks off."

Eden laughed. "We talked about you."

His expression shifted toward wariness. "Oh, yeah?"

"Yes, but he wasn't matchmaking. He said that he was taking these lessons only so you'd learn to cook healthy food and not have a heart attack."

This smile, unlike his earlier polite ones, reached his eyes, crinkling the corners, transforming his face. Damn.

"I left my number on the notepad on the kitchen counter in case you need me."

"Great." He held the door for her and then walked with her as far as his SUV, which he'd parked on the street behind her car. "I'll give you a call to set up a time tonight or tomorrow to go over the operation of the system."

"Sounds good," she called, getting into her car.

She hummed to herself as she started the engine, watching Nick in the rearview mirror.

Hot guy.

Confidence builder.

THE FIRST ORDER of business was to get at the computer. She only had one, a desktop in her bedroom. Nick powered it up and inserted the startup disk that would allow him to bypass her password. As soon as he had access, he downloaded the files onto the memory stick. While the little light at the end of the stick blinked, he went back into the living room and begin unpacking boxes, thinking about Eden.

He honestly hoped she wasn't involved in any kind of a crime. He'd run the vehicle identification number on her brother's Firebird, which Nick had gotten the night of the cooking lesson, and found that he'd bought it locally from a guy who ran the entertainment segment for the Cassandra Hotel chain, which included the Tahoe Summit. He didn't know if it was paid for in cash, as drug dealers tended to do, or whether Justin had financed it.

Nick hoped the purchase was aboveboard and financed, and that bothered him. Staying removed from his subjects allowed him to view evidence dispassionately, to not be swayed by emotion. Right now he was being swayed.

Not good.

A few minutes later he pocketed the memory stick. The reason he'd come here was accomplished. Now for all the bullshit he needed to do to cover his tracks.

He started with the security system, since he wanted to get that up and running first. Installation was just as easy and uneventful as the instructions had promised. He drilled a few holes for mounting and to run the wiring through, clamped the monitor onto the bracket and voilà— it looked as if a pro had done it. Next came the window locks and then he'd mount the sensors.

Fortunately, Eden lived in a small house without that many windows, so drilling holes in the sashes for the dead bolts was also easier than he'd thought it would be. Maybe this could be his second career. If he didn't start getting along with the lieutenant, it might well be his main one.

He worked his way through the house, finishing in her bedroom. There was a pile of silky underwear and nightgowns under the window and he edged it aside with the toe of his shoe, only to hit something hard. And flat. He leaned down to push the clothing aside.

A laptop.

Shit.

Nick went back to the front room to retrieve the startup disk, glad he'd stumbled upon the second computer, and feeling a bit stupid for not finding it earlier. He'd checked all the usual places. Areas around chairs and beds, on desks and tables, near outlets. Looking under a pile of lingerie hadn't occurred to him. In fact, he'd avoided the heap.

He powered up the machine, put in the disk and started the download. Once he made sure it was working, he raised the drill to finish the two windows in her bedroom. He'd just started his second-to-last hole when the sound of the front door opening and closing startled the piss out of him, and the drill slipped, raking down the edge of his hand.

"Nick? It's me."

Eden. Holy...

He dumped the lingerie back on the laptop without closing the lid, since he didn't know if the download was complete, arranging the pile as best he could before starting for the kitchen to intercept her. He just hoped the silk undies didn't catch fire from the heat of the machine.

"UH, HI," NICK said, coming into the kitchen from the hall at the same time Eden entered from the living room. "I didn't expect you back until later."

"Yeah, I know." She put her purse down on the table. "Justin is covering for me on his day off."

Nick cocked his head. "Doesn't sound like much of a day off."

Eden laughed and lifted the canvas bag she carried onto the counter. "Cooks cook."

"That's the way it is with you?" he asked.

"Mmm-hmm. Which is why I'm going to make you lunch."

An odd expression played over Nick's face. "Oh, no. You don't have to—"

Eden walked across the kitchen to where he stood with a hammer in one hand and a drill in the other, stopping a couple feet in front of him and facing off like a gunfighter. "Cooks cook. And they love it. I'm cooking for you."

He swallowed. "All right. Since it seems that there's no stopping you."

"There isn't," she assured him. She looked down at his hand. "Are you bleeding?"

"It's nothing," he said. "The drill slipped. Stupid of me."

"Let me get you a Band-Aid."

"No. I have one in my tool kit. I'll go get it. Don't want to drip on your floor." He smiled at her, then quickly turned and walked out of the kitchen and down the hall to her bedroom, where he must have been working.

Eden pulled the fresh produce out of the bag along with a baguette and a tin of tuna fish. She peeled and crushed a couple cloves of garlic, placed them in a glass dish and covered them with olive oil.

Once the oil was being flavored, she went to inspect the security system's control panel next to her pantry door. It looked very high-tech and intimidating. She reached out to run a finger over the panel. In a way she was sad that her life had come to this—alarms and such—but better safe and a touch sad than sorry.

Heavy footsteps sounded down the hall and Nick walked into the room, a bandage on his finger.

"Is this easy to use?" she asked.

"Very simple." He came over to stand close to her. "You press a code to arm it and a code to disarm. You have a delay, so you can do it after coming into the house. I don't have the sensors mounted yet. I'm working on the dead bolts."

She shrugged. "Well, don't let me slow you down. I'll make lunch and let you know when it's ready."

THE MEMORY STICK was deep in Nick's pocket, the startup disk in one of the boxes he was about to carry out to the SUV. He just hoped Eden didn't try to use her computer in the next few minutes, or she might notice how hot it was from running while sitting under a pile of silky underwear.

He decided to abandon the window locks for now, while the computer cooled, and work in the kitchen, installing the dead bolt in the back door. He pulled the instructions from his pocket and took a look while he was outside, then went back into the kitchen with his drill and a chisel in one hand, the lock in the other. *Mark the faceplate. Drill holes. Mark where the dead bolt will protrude from edge of door, drill and chisel.*

He mentally repeated the instructions one more time. They really weren't that difficult and the diagrams were quite clear. Piece of cake.

Eden was pulling the soft part of the bread out of a long loaf, leaving only the crust, when he walked into the kitchen. She dumped the bread in the trash.

"I would have eaten that," he said, opening

the back door. No remnant dead bolt hole from an earlier lock. Damn.

"The sandwich will be better." She started brushing oil over the crust, then spreading tuna down the loaf. Nick stopped and watched.

"What're you making? The world's longest tuna sandwich?"

She smiled without looking up. "I am. It's called pan bagnat."

"Which is French for long tuna fish sandwich?" He took the pencil out of his shirt pocket and drew around the faceplate.

"Close. I think it has more to do with the Niçoise olives."

"Nee-*swahz* olives," he echoed pompously, pulling the chisel out of his tool belt.

Eden laughed and started putting rings of purple onion on the sandwich, followed by capers and olives—possibly Niçoise. Nick drilled a hole in each corner of the faceplate outline, then lowered his drill and watched as she opened a jar of roasted red peppers. This sandwich had definite possibilities.

He positioned the chisel and gave it a tap with the hammer. It practically bounced off the door. Okay. A little harder.

"Is this an oak door?" he asked.

"I wouldn't be surprised," she said. "It could be anything under all those layers of paint. It is an older house."

"Well, I guess that explains why there wasn't already a dead bolt in it." He hit the chisel harder and managed to get a toehold in the wood. He hit it again and it went deeper. He pushed down on the chisel, prying out the hunk of wood. It moved. A little. He pushed harder. It moved a little more. Then suddenly the chisel gave and flipped through the air, the heavy handle hitting him square between the eyes.

He staggered backward, more out of surprise than pain, his hand clamped to his face. "Son of a bitch!"

"Nick!" Eden dropped a spoon with a clatter. "Let me see."

"No." He waved her away. "I'm fine. Just… startled." And embarrassed. He slowly lowered his hand, checked the palm for blood, just in case. Nothing. He was damned lucky not to have been hit by the business end.

"Aren't you supposed to be wearing safety glasses?"

"Excellent point." He didn't have any safety glasses. What a professional he was. "I left them in the car."

"Maybe you should go get them?" Eden asked as he pressed his hand to his forehead again. "After I get you some ice."

"I don't need ice."

"You're getting ice. Sit down." She motioned to one of her chairs. Bemused, Nick sat down. "You can get the glasses later."

She went to her freezer and pulled out a small package of frozen peas, which she handed to him. He took the bag and slapped it onto his face.

"Happy?" he asked.

"Very glad I'm not wiping up blood."

"That makes two of us." He looked at her from the eye that wasn't covered by frozen peas. "This is a little embarrassing."

She didn't try to make him feel better. "It should be. You were almost taken out by your own tool."

Kind of like shooting yourself in the foot, which Marcus had almost done once on the range.

"Stay there," she said sternly as she went back to the counter, "and let the ice work for a couple minutes. I'll finish the sandwich and we can eat, then you can get back to work."

Nick nodded and closed his eyes. The cold bag felt good, the situation did not. He had the data, which he would look at tonight, but he felt crappy about stealing it.

No. He felt crappy because Eden charmed him and he didn't want her to be involved in criminal activities. Even by association.

"I'm supposed to wrap this sandwich and let the flavors develop, but I think we'll skip that part," she said. He opened his eye to see her brandishing a giant knife. What was it about this woman and knives?

A moment later she set a plate in front of him with a healthy portion of the French tuna sandwich. "You might want to put this back in the freezer," he said, handing her the bag of peas.

"Yes," she said innocently. "You still have to get that hole in the door finished."

Don't play along. Don't do it.

He narrowed his eyes at her. "Maybe you'd like to help?"

She put a hand to her chest in mock horror. "I don't want to get anywhere near you and a tool after that display." Her expression grew more serious. "But maybe you should drill a few more holes."

"That was my next official move," he said, taking a giant bite of a most excellent sandwich. "I was trying to save a step."

"And you'll get your safety glasses? Just in case…"

"Of course." A sudden thought struck him. He had shooting glasses in the SUV. Good to go. She wouldn't notice Winchester written on the upper part of the lenses. He hoped. She was pretty sharp.

NICK FINISHED PUTTING the dead bolt in the back door without incident, and drilled a lot more holes before he attempted to chisel out the space for the mechanism in the front door. He also wore his safety glasses. Eden stayed back and allowed him to work, although she wasn't above studying him from a distance.

When he finished installing the motion sensors and the window locks, it was almost two o'clock. He walked her through the process for arming and disarming the system.

"Is there a possibility of false alarms?"

"Yes. But always assume that it's for real. Okay?"

"Oh, I will," she said with feeling.

"Not a lot of point having a security system if you ignore the alarms the way you'd started to ignore the motion sensor light. And if that thing comes on—"

"It's not a cat."

"Not a cat," he agreed, hooking his thumb in his tool belt. She did love a man in a tool belt.

"Or a bear."

He'd started to stack the boxes together to take with him when Eden said, "I can take care of that."

"Part of the service." He jammed a bunch of small boxes and plastic bags into one of the larger boxes. "None of my business," he said when he was done, "but have you had any more visits from your ex?"

"No visits," Eden said. Ian was finally part of her past. She walked with Nick as far as the door. "I'll see you next Wednesday."

"Wednesday." He smiled, the corners of his eyes crinkling pleasantly as he looked down at her, but there was something in his expression she couldn't quite read. Something that looked just a bit like regret.

CHAPTER EIGHT

"WELL, IT LOOKS like you went to all this trouble for nothing," Marcus said dismissively, pushing the memory sticks across the coffee shop table in a way that made Nick want to pop him. He wouldn't, though. Marcus was the reason he'd wasted the whole frigging day pretending to be a security expert—although the little worm had yet to fess up to rock throwing. But he would. Eventually. The guy was playing holier than thou, but he liked credit.

The accountant squinted slightly as he studied Nick's face. "How'd you get that bruise between your eyes?"

"Long story," Nick said. And kind of a funny one, really. Or it would be with time. Maybe it hadn't been a totally wasted day. He'd eaten an excellent sandwich and spent some time with a woman he found interesting. A woman he really shouldn't find interesting, but did.

He tapped a memory stick with one finger. "Nothing at all?"

Marcus leaned back in his chair. "I was able to access her bank account, but no. Nothing."

Nick felt a twinge of relief even as the logical part of his brain told him all that meant was records weren't on Eden's home computer and her personal bank account wasn't involved in a crime. It didn't mean her brother was clean.

He leaned back in his chair, mirroring Marcus. "Did you throw the rock through Eden's window?"

Marcus simply sneered at him. "What are you going to do now?"

Nick held up the memory sticks before pocketing them. "I want to either cross these guys off the list or be in a position to squeeze Tremont hard."

"If Justin Tremont doesn't end up being your 'in,' what are you going to do?" the accountant asked.

Nick didn't want to think about that. If Tremont was clean, then he'd be very happy in some regards and at a total dead as far as the investigation went.

Cully would go unavenged, unless something

broke, and the drugs would continue to move through the Tahoe Summit.

EDEN DROPPED HER meals off a little earlier than usual that Sunday. Patty had had nothing on her prep list from Justin, so she'd been able to help cook and portion out the dinners.

The Stewart house was Eden's first stop, and she parked next to the giant stucco garage and let herself in with a key. The Stewarts kept a huge freezer and two fridges in the garage—a lot of cold storage for a family that didn't cook. But Eden was more than happy to fill those fridges in exchange for a healthy paycheck.

The Ballard house was not far away and Eden usually preferred delivering there, since Tina was almost always home Sunday evening and liked to chat, sometimes over a glass of wine.

Eden was so early in her delivery today, though, that only the two boys, Jed and Joshua, were home. Jed answered the back door when she knocked and actually smiled at her.

"Hey, scuzz," he called to his brother. "Come and help."

Joshua came through the arched kitchen

doorway and obligingly took the box he shoved at him.

"There are two coolers in the back of the van," Eden said.

"Ready for the big shindig?" Josh asked, tipping back a bottle of beer.

"I can't believe you're old enough to drink," she said as she unloaded the box. He'd been sixteen when she'd started cooking for them. "And yes, I'm ready."

Jed came in with a cooler and, knowing the drill, started unloading. Eden wondered if Rosemary would grow up this quickly. She hoped not.

Once both coolers were empty, Jed hauled one out to the car for her. Eden couldn't help but notice that he was a lot more personable when his mother wasn't around.

Teens were rugged. She knew. She'd helped raise Justin.

"Guess I'll see you next week."

"And the Tuesday after that," Eden said.

"Because no one throws parties on a Tuesday," Jed said with a touch of gentle sarcasm.

It was still daylight when Eden got home, but even so, she had to admit she felt a lot safer going into the house with the alarm system in place. She also hadn't realized how often the old motion sensors had come on until she'd spent an uninterrupted evening.

In fact, she began to wonder if the lights even worked, and went outside to test them herself. She skulked behind the bushes Justin had trimmed back for her, and sure enough, the lights came on. Her home was secure.

Her newfound sense of security lasted one more night. On the third evening she was experimenting with a puree made of roasted vegetables when the alarm went off, scaring the bejeezus out of her. She debated about calling the police, except that it was still daylight. No doors or windows were compromised and her neighbor across the alley was outside, taking her laundry, which was whipping wildly in the wind, off the line.

False alarm. Eden reset the system. Glitches were to be expected. She was simply glad it hadn't happened at night. Then she would have called the police and it would probably have *been* a false alarm. She would have felt like a fool.

The alarm went off a second time when she was in the shower, trying to beat the lightning storm approaching. Never shower in a lightning storm was one of her father's few rules—a sure sign he'd cared.... Regardless, it was a rule Eden followed.

She traipsed to the control box, giant towel wrapped around her, and found the circumstances the same as before. Nothing appeared compromised and there were kids out on the street riding bikes, papers and leaves blowing around them as the storm brewed.

A storm shouldn't affect the system. One more false alarm and Nick would have to investigate. Eden had a feeling she would not be able to convince herself all was well if the alarm went off in the dead of the night.

NICK WAS SPRAWLED in front of his TV, watching *Cops* and wondering about the best way to get at the Tremont records when his phone rang. He didn't recognize the number, but as soon as he answered, he recognized the voice.

"I'm sorry to bother you," Eden said with a touch of annoyance, "but I've had three false alarms this evening and I'm getting a little tired of it."

Shit. He let his head fall back against the sofa. "You're sure they're false?"

"Either that or I have a persistent home invader who doesn't set off motion sensor lights and isn't particularly bothered by alarms."

"Okay. I'll be right over." Just as soon as he had time to do some research.

Forty minutes later, he parked in front of her house, cursing Marcus. Rock through the window. And for nothing.

The wind caught his truck door as he opened it, and he was barely able to hold on to it. Nasty storm blowing in, which he hoped was the solution to his problem. If it wasn't, then he was going to have to conjure up some BS about contacting the company rep, etc.

Eden opened the door before he reached the top step, grasping the lapels of a lavender satin robe as she ducked her head against the wind.

"No tool belt?" she said as he stepped inside and she slammed the door shut.

He lifted the small canvas toolbox. "More comfortable," he said with a half smile before inspecting the control panel as if he had any idea what he was doing.

He checked the wiring connections, which were both good, tested the backup batteries with the gauge he'd bought on the way over.

"And?" Eden asked, still clutching the robe, which he could see now wasn't sleepwear, but rather a kimono.

He looked down at her and raised his eyebrows

in a candid expression. "Honestly? I'm new at this. I think it might have something to do with the wind hitting the windows and rattling the connections on the sensors."

"So when the wind blows I'll have false alarms? If so, then I need to rethink this."

"I'm going to try to adjust the sensors." Which he did, following the instructions on the system troubleshooting site. "I'm going to refund some of your money for this."

"Really?"

"Like I said, I'm new and you shouldn't pay for my mistakes."

"As near as I can tell, I didn't pay you much more than the cost of the components."

"I get a good deal from my supplier."

She gave a soft snort. "Must be a really good deal."

After he was done "adjusting"—and he had found a couple loose connections—he turned on the system, tested it, then let it settle into working mode. For a moment he and Eden stood there; she was focused on the panel and he was focused on her. She gave him a quick sideways glance.

"Do you want a beer while you wait?"

"Wait for what?"

She finally let go of the front of the kimono

and he saw why she'd been holding it—so as not to distract him from his job. "Wait to see if there's another false alarm. Either that or I'm calling you when it happens again."

"Yeah?" he said, dropping his screwdriver into the canvas bag.

"I appreciate you putting it in for me, but I did pay for a service, and being a businessperson myself, I expect to get what I pay for."

No arguing with that. "I'd love a beer."

"Light or dark?"

He perked up. "You have both?"

She made a face at him. "Of course."

"Dark."

She waved at the sofa. "Have a seat."

Nick sat and looked around the living room. He actually knew this house pretty well now. Eden favored silky fabrics and muted colors. Kind of at odds with her personality.

She came back into the living room, the kimono swishing around her legs as she walked, and handed him one of two opened oatmeal stouts before sitting down beside him. She put her feet up on the coffee table and took a long draw of her beer.

Nick started laughing.

"What?" she asked, dabbing at her damp lips with her fingertips.

"Nothing. It's just…" He smiled, realizing that he seemed to smile a lot around her. A lot more than he had around anyone, except maybe Daphne, in the past few years.

"It's just…?" Eden echoed, gesturing with her beer to encourage him.

"You're this small, feminine—"

"Don't you dare say perky."

He shook his head, seeing the spark in her very blue eyes. "Wasn't going to say perky."

She focused on the dark television screen on the opposite side of the room. "Everyone does."

"Calls you perky?"

"I think I first heard the phrase in the fourth grade. And it snowballed from there."

He set his bottle on his thigh, keeping his fingers wrapped around the neck. "There's nothing wrong with perky."

She turned, leaning one shoulder into the sofa cushions as she looked him square in the eye. "Would you like to be called that?"

"No."

She rolled back to her original position, presenting him once again with her profile. "Well, there you go."

He shook his head and took a drink of his beer. "What I was about to say was that I like your style. Feet on the coffee table, cold beer, remote at the ready."

"Justin taught me well," she said in an off-hand way, unknowingly splashing cold water on an otherwise enjoyable conversation. "Besides, I believe in being comfortable."

Nick could see that. Everything in her house was homey and inviting. The way her kimono was draped at the moment was rather inviting, too, in a very different way. It'd been so long since he'd been with a woman. First because of the grief, and then because he'd buried himself in his cases and had no time. It wasn't until he'd opened his big fat mouth that he'd found himself with time on his hands.

"You're not at home much, are you?" he said.

"Not lately. I'm kind of swamped without my sister and would be totally in the weeds if it wasn't for Patty and a couple reliable temps."

"What about your brother?"

She took a drink of her beer, leaving small beads of moisture on her lower lip. "One of the chefs at the hotel where Justin works got injured in a motorcycle accident, and he's filling in."

"Must have put a crimp in the cake business," Nick said, focusing back on his bottle.

"He's not in a position to say no, if he wants to keep working at the hotel—which he does, since he gets a lot of contacts through the casino and he has an in with one of the wedding chapels up there."

Nick wondered where else he might have an in. He was driving one hell of a car and spent almost half his working life at a place with known drug ties.

"It should only be for another week or two." She adjusted her kimono, closing the V a little more. "I see you've recovered from your security installation," she said, her gaze zeroing in on his fingers.

Nick glanced down at his hands. This was the first day he hadn't worn a bandage.

She was smiling at him over the top of her beer bottle. Laughing at him, really. And, in a way, challenging him.

"Let me see *your* hands."

"Why?" she asked, startled.

Nick reached out, took the bottle from her and set it on the coffee table, then gently grasped her hands. "So we can compare scars."

He held her right hand up, inspecting her fingers. There were numerous small scars. Some barely visible, because they'd been clean slices like his. Several small nicks. The crisscrossed X on her index finger she'd shown him earlier. There was another nasty one in the crease between her thumb and forefinger.

"How'd you get that?" he asked softly.

"Serrated knife. Long time ago."

"Cooking school?"

"No. Home. I was cutting a box for a school project and slipped with the knife." She slid her fingers between his, linking their hands, locking them together. It felt…good. Good enough that he wasn't going to spend time analyzing where they were heading with this. The sofa, the beer. The wind buffeting the windows. They all made the small house even more intimate.

"Why weren't you using a box cutter?"

She shrugged. "We didn't have a lot of tools around. Not much supervision, either. Reggie had to hunt my dad down in another state to get a verbal to treat me at the emergency room. We tried to close it up ourselves with butterflies, but we just couldn't get the job done."

"Why was your dad in another state?"

"He was a long-haul trucker. Couldn't get

enough of the open road." There was definite bitterness in her voice.

"Didn't spend much time at home?"

"He popped in for the occasional holiday." Eden's expression grew somber, a touch more vulnerable, and Nick realized her "perkiness" might be a bit of a shield.

She looked down at their still-linked hands, then leaned over and very softly kissed his mouth, her lips lingering just long enough to give him a hint of what she could offer.

It was the first time he'd been kissed by a woman since losing Miri. Two years—time that had dragged on in some respects and raced forward in others.

Eden eased back, letting her head rest on the cushions again, her eyes half-closed, and that was when he realized he was hanging on to her hand for dear life.

When he loosened his grip she slid her fingers free and gave him a gentle smile.

"One beer and no false alarm. I think you fixed the system."

EDEN HAD NEVER in her life hoped she might have a false alarm of any kind, but she wouldn't mind curling up on a sofa again with Nick. Or kissing him.

Once he'd driven away, she turned off the lights and started for her bedroom. A little response would have been nice, but she'd taken him by surprise—though why, she had no idea, because she thought she'd been giving him some decent signals. And he'd wanted to respond; she could feel it when she'd kissed him. But he'd held back.

Too much, too soon?

Maybe.

But she sensed that they honestly had a good connection between them. Different from anything she'd experienced before. And there was something else about him that she couldn't quite put her finger on. A feeling of weariness or sadness. As if he'd been knocked around a bit by life.

Well, he'd been a cop and cops saw a lot. Maybe Nick had seen a little too much. Maybe that was why he was no longer active.

NICK KEPT THINKING about Eden kissing him. He shouldn't have been sitting on her sofa, holding her hand like a teenager, but it had felt...right. And when she'd kissed him, he could have so easily pulled her onto his lap and spent a very long time slowly exploring her mouth, caressing her body. Not doing that, walking away, had to have been one the hardest things he'd done recently—aside from not killing Marcus.

Nick was rinsing his cereal bowl early Wednesday morning when Daphne called. Since it wasn't time for her to be at work, and she never went in early unless it was an emergency, he had a bad feeling

"They found Cully," she said.

Nick rubbed a hand over his forehead, knowing the answer to his question before he asked. "Dead?"

"Yeah."

"Who found him? And where?"

"Search and rescue, during a training last night. He, or what was left of him, was at the bottom of an abandoned mine shaft near Portner Summit."

"Accident?" he asked. People did sometimes explore old mines and fall into shafts—although Cully had not come off as that kind of guy.

"Bullet in the skull. A .38 caliber."

Nick let out a breath. He'd truly had a soft spot for the kid.

"I'm going to talk to the lieutenant," Daphne said. "Cully disappeared just before the meeting about the Summit drug-money laundering. I want to see if I can convince him there's a tie-in."

Of course there was. "Careful you don't get suspended," Nick said. She snorted, but it was halfhearted.

He hung up the phone and then tossed it onto the counter. Shit. He'd known Cully was dead; could see no other possibility. But now that his death was confirmed, it truly made Nick furious. He wanted to hang the guy who'd done this up by his nuts.

Right now, the only person Nick had access to was Justin Tremont, and he was damn well going to see what the guy knew. If he was pushing money through the catering business, Nick was going to find out. If he wasn't, then Nick would question him about what he did know. He couldn't be working in that kitchen and not be aware that many of the employees had extracurricular careers.

Nick was just sorry that Eden and Justin were related.

NICK ARRIVED AT the kitchen early that night instead of following the van from the Candlewood Center. He had to get his hands on a key, just for a minute or two, and with the old guys keeping

Eden busy, he should be able to do it. If he could get into the office. That was the tricky part.

The front door was open and the reception area dim, as it always was when the kitchen was closed. The computer was off and there was no music coming through the wall from the room where Justin worked on whatever he did. Nick walked over to the desk and quickly checked all the drawers, in case there was a spare set of keys. A wild shot, but sometimes it paid off.

Nothing. He headed for the kitchen, pausing at the entrance.

Eden's back was to him as she read over some notecards scattered across the top of one of the stainless-steel counters, and the first thing he noticed was that her skirt was shorter than usual. Nothing indecent, but it showed more of her legs. Damned fine legs, to go with the very fine cleavage he'd gotten flashes of the other night.

He raised his hand to knock on the door frame, to let her know he was there, but at the last second lowered it back to his side. The more time he spent hanging around this place, and Eden, the more certain he was that there was nothing illegal going on—Tremont was solely a catering business.

Or was that just the way he wanted things to be?

Finally, he cleared his throat and she turned. "I didn't know anyone was here," she said, her blue eyes wide.

"Yeah, I know," he said, coming into the kitchen. "Sorry about that."

"My fault. I turned the buzzer off on the front door and didn't turn it on again." She pushed her hair back over her shoulders. For once it was down instead of up in a knot, and he liked how it fell partway down her back. Soft. Silky. Touchable. He closed his hands into fists.

"How's the system behaving?"

She smiled and some of her natural sparkle came back into her face. "No false alarms. And I saw the cats go by last night, but they don't set off the motion sensors."

"Any bears?"

Eden laughed. "No bears. Much to my brother's disappointment."

There was a loud bang on the front door as someone knocked, which Nick should have done instead of startling her.

Lois came in first, followed by Lenny and Paul. Marcus traipsed behind, which surprised Nick. He figured that once Marcus's mission was done, once he'd gotten Nick "in," he would back off. But no. He seemed to like the lessons. Seemed to enjoy being top of the class.

Maybe he was like Nick and didn't know a hell of a lot about cooking. Whatever, Nick was feeling a bit more kindly toward him after their last discussion. He and Daphne were not the only ones wondering why their case had been dumped.

"Instead of French toast, we're making meat loaf tonight, since there was extra ground sirloin from last week's chili lesson," Eden explained. "And since we don't have an hour and a half to wait for the meat loaf to bake, we're going to make it into meatballs."

"I love meatballs," Lenny said in his gravelly voice. He looked over at Marcus. "How about you, kid?"

"Yes," Marcus said in a monotone. "I love a meatball."

"I have recipe cards for all of you. This is a very simple procedure. You can use the precut onion like last time, or cut your own."

"I'm not cutting jack," Gabe said. "My joints are bugging me."

"I'll do it," Nick offered. He frowned slightly. "Are you all right?"

"Fine," he said. "Just a little heartburn."

Nick didn't like the sound of that. "Heartburn."

"What'd I just say?" Gabe demanded. "And it makes me irritable, so watch out."

"No, shit," Nick said. "But you're sure it's heartburn?"

Gabe shot him a fiery look just as Eden passed by.

"Here's the recipe. I'm going to have you guys follow along with me." She smiled warmly at Gabe, arched her eyebrows at Nick and then turned to address the crowd.

"First, if you're dicing onions, make them pretty fine. You'll also need to peel one carrot and grate it."

"Are you sure that meatballs are supposed to have carrots in them?" James asked, holding the recipe up to his face in spite of his overly thick glasses.

"Adds sweetness and moisture," Lois said.

Nick peeled the onion and started slicing while Gabe scraped the carrot. "No," Nick said. "Put the point down on the counter and then peel."

"What the—?" Gabe shook his head, but jammed the end of the carrot down onto the counter as Eden approached. Sure enough, the peeler glided smoothly down the carrot, which was no longer bobbing up and down with each stroke.

"Where'd you learn to peel carrots?" Gabe asked.

"Eden taught me—oh, shit!" Nick's knife clattered to the counter.

CHAPTER NINE

EDEN DID HATE to hear that sound. "How bad?" she asked mildly, wondering if Nick remembered what she'd said about blood flowing freely in a kitchen.

"It's...a pretty good one," he said, holding his index finger in his other hand.

She gestured with her head to the rear of the kitchen, where they had one basin dedicated to nonfood items and injuries.

"Let's see," she said once they were there. She took hold of his wrist and pulled his hands over the sink. As soon as he took the pressure off his finger, blood immediately started dripping into the sink, mixing with the thin stream of water she'd turned on. "Take hold of it again and press hard. We need to stop the flow long enough to get a gauze pad on it.... Are you left-handed?"

He looked at her with a perplexed expression. "No. Why?"

"Statistics show that left-handed people have more accidents. First the chisel, now this."

"You want to let me take a look at your hands again?" Nick growled. "I seem to remember a scar or two."

Ignoring him, even though the growl did things to her insides, she took the first-aid kit out of the cupboard over the basin and found the gauze. Then she slipped on a pair of latex gloves like a surgeon about to tackle an operation.

"Wait...aren't *you* left-handed?" he asked.

She shot him a quick look before taking hold of his hand. "Very observant. Okay, let go."

As soon as he released pressure, Eden started wrapping his finger. At first blood seeped through the white gauze, but by the time she'd mummified the finger, there was no red stain, probably because she'd just about cut off his circulation. She secured the gauze with a strip of white tape, then stepped away from the warm masculine scent that was driving her nuts.

"It's going to bleed through pretty soon," she said. "Let me know if it gets too bad and we'll change it out."

"Will do," he said, although she doubted it. He had stoic written all over him.

"Last thing," she said, holding up a latex finger

sheath. He drew back slightly and then held out his hand, watching her warily as she rolled the sheath down over his injury, and tried not to think what it reminded her of.

"Good to go," she said, trying to look unaffected by the direction her thoughts had taken.

"Thank you," he said gravely.

"You're welcome," Eden said with equal gravity. She washed her hands, and when she turned back to her class she found at least six sets of eyes focused on her and Nick. They quickly went back to their cooking, and Eden let out a breath.

Lovely. Just lovely.

"DID YOU DO that on purpose?" Gabe asked when Nick returned to their station.

He stopped in his tracks. "What?"

"You know…just to get some attention?"

He shook his head in disgust. "I'm not six, and if I want Eden's attention, I'll come up with a way that doesn't involve blood. You know, like, say, hiding my wallet."

Gabe snorted. "Just checking." He gave the beef mixture a final stir. "I guess I have to make the meatballs, since you're on the injured list."

"Guess so," Nick replied mildly. Eden was

helping Marcus form the correct size meatballs, since his could be used to play tennis.

"We want them to cook through," Nick heard her say.

"How's this look for size?" Gabe asked, holding up a misshapen ball.

"Not bad." His grandfather grunted and continued to form the mixture with his arthritic hands. "I can help," Nick said.

"I want to do it," Gabe replied. "I might make these at home."

Blood was showing through the gauze on Nick's finger by the time the meatballs were in the oven and Eden was explaining how to put them in a pan and cover them with tomato sauce to warm on the stove once they got home.

He held on to his finger and silently crossed the kitchen to the sink, taking the first-aid kit off the shelf. A second later he carried it into the tiny office and sat down in one of the chairs in front of the computers. Great. He opened the kit and placed it on the other chair, then nudged the door with his toe so it half closed.

As soon as the door blocked him from view, he started opening drawers. He was beginning to think he was going to have to dig through her purse when he saw a set of keys next to the computer monitor, half covered by a folder.

He pulled his phone out of his pocket and laid the keys out, photographing the two that weren't obvious car keys. Then he pushed them back under the folder and pocketed the phone before reaching for the gauze.

Mission accomplished.

LOIS AND THE guys helped tidy up the kitchen, then said their farewells. Gabe walked with his grandfather as far as the van.

"That finger doesn't need stitches, does it?"

"Hardly," Nick said. Or so he hoped. He'd sliced deeper than he'd intended, and it hurt like hell.

"Then why is that balloon on your finger full of blood?"

Nick raised his finger and grimaced.

"All you gotta do," Lenny said, leaning forward to look out the sliding van door, "is dip your finger in a little gasoline. That stops a bleed every time."

"I'll, uh, keep that in mind," Nick said. The van door closed a few seconds later and he waited until it pulled away before he turned back to his

SUV. Eden was standing in the open doorway, watching him.

"You're still here," she said, one corner of her mouth curved up slightly, reminding him of the way she'd smiled after she'd kissed him. A Mona Lisa–type smile.

"Yeah. I often go to the center and spend some time with the guys, and Wednesday is a good night to do it. Two birds with one stone. We talk about the cooking lesson and play poker."

"But not tonight."

"Not tonight," he agreed. Tonight he wanted to go home and be alone for a while. Try to ignore the you're-an-asshole feeling eating at him.

"How's the finger?"

He pushed his hand slightly behind him so she couldn't see that the sheath was full of blood. "I'll live. I learned an important lesson."

"Which is?"

"Keep you fingers curled back."

"Where have I heard that?" she asked, reaching out to open the door. "I have to close up."

"Your brother isn't coming in tonight?"

She shook her head.

Nick took a couple slow steps toward her, his footsteps echoing on the asphalt. "Why don't I wait until you're done?"

"A safety issue?"

"That's part of it," he said. Another part… could he possibly unlock the back door without her knowing it, slip in later tonight and thus avoid having the key made? Due to the open layout of the kitchen, probably not, but he'd give it a shot.

But that wasn't the only reason he was hanging around. He didn't like leaving Eden alone in the kitchen afterhours—or to have her walk to her car in the empty lot.

She smiled again in that intriguing way she had when she was tired, then gestured with her head. "Come on in. I just have to make sure everything is turned off and locked up."

Nick waited next to the office while she checked the stoves, made certain the refrigerators were closed, the back door locked.

"How'd Justin ever get into this pastry-baking game?" he asked. "Did he always like to bake?"

"Hardly," Eden said, taking off her apron and hanging it on a hook next to a bank of lockers. She smoothed her hands down over her red dress. "He spent most of his teen years tinkering with cars when he wasn't at school."

"So how'd he…?"

"We all took turns cooking when my dad was gone, which was pretty much all the time, and he discovered that girls liked guys who could cook. Then he got a job with the same catering company that gave me my start. He found out he liked cooking and food as much as Reggie and I do, so he went to cooking school, too."

"Did he abandon the cars?"

She looked up at him as if surprised he'd even mention such a possibility, "Oh, no. Surely you've noticed his pride and joy parked in a place of honor in the front lot."

"The Firebird?"

"That's the one," Eden said. "When he's not driving it, he's tinkering with it or polishing it."

"How'd he get it? Those cars are hard to find."

"Nepotism and scheming," she said with a laugh.

"Yeah?"

"I cook weekly meals for the guy in charge of entertainment at the Summit Hotel in Tahoe and the Cassandra in Reno."

"Private chef?"

"In a way. I make four days of meals that are easy to reheat to help them get through the week. Friday through Sunday, they're on their own."

"I might need to hire you," Nick said.

"You're taking cooking lessons," she reminded him.

"Anyway, about the car…" He gave her a half smile.

"Yes, the car." Eden pushed a partially open locker door shut. "Sometimes Justin delivers the meals for me, and one time he spotted the Firebird in Michael's garage. It was love at first sight. It took two years of hints, offers and shameless begging before Michael sold it to him."

"Persistence pays, I guess."

"It did this time. And I owe Michael because until Justin bought it, he had this awful old junker parked at my house. He sold it to help pay for the Firebird."

She crossed to the door next to the office. "I just need to check the thermostat. We keep this room cooler for the pastry work."

Nick followed her. "Is he working on a cake now?"

"Want to see?" Eden said. Without waiting for an answer, she opened the door with a flourish. For a moment Nick simply stared.

The cake sitting on a stainless-steel table in the middle of the cold room was four layers high and at least three feet across. The pale yellow layers had an elaborate design of different playing cards—kings, queens, jacks and aces in various suits—that appeared to be drawn directly onto the icing with red, black and gold frosting.

How could a guy who liked to work on cars make a cake like that?

"One of the casino execs is getting married, and this is what they wanted for their cake." Eden wrinkled her nose slightly and Nick had to agree with her. The cake was magnificent, but not exactly traditional wedding material.

He slowly circled the structure, taking in the detail. Justin Tremont was a true artist. "It's... big."

"Yes. Justin has to travel with the cake to set it up, and we have to make certain someone is there who knows how to dismantle it for serving. There's a lot of supports inside the cake, holding it up."

"How long does it take to make something like this?"

"Days. And sometimes more days on top of that, if there's some kind of disaster."

Nick turned back to her. "Does he do a lot of these?"

"Yes, he does. He's developed a decent reputation. He's artistic and delivers on time, although we've had a lot of nail-biters."

"A cake like this must be damned expensive."

"More than I'd pay. In the thousands."

"Thousands? I was thinking hundreds."

"Not for the amount of work Justin puts in. There's a formula he uses that involves number of tiers and diameter, etc. Anyway, in my mind he earns every penny."

Nick leaned his hip against the counter. "Do you ever lend a hand?"

Eden snorted. "As if. For one thing, Justin is really territorial. For another, I don't have time. And I'm bad at piping and flowers. He'll let me roll fondant and make butter cream, but that's the extent of my contribution."

She motioned with her head toward the door. "Speaking of which, Justin can sense when someone has been in his lair."

Nick laughed, but he also wondered if Eden had the same ability.

"I need to get home," she said, walking to the office, where she made a search for her keys before locating them under the folder, right where Nick had found them. She gathered up her purse and a pale blue sweater, turned off the office lights and glanced up at him.

The atmosphere between them practically crackled. Nick swallowed and started resolutely toward the entrance. No crackling tonight.

He held open the front door and she walked under his arm, fitting the key into the lock once the door had swung shut. And now that he knew which key went to the front—the stubby one—he also had a very good idea which key went to the back.

Eden walked to her car, a small red Honda that almost matched her dress, with slow steps, as if she didn't want to get there too fast. The night was warm, with a touch of humidity. Unusual for Reno in late March, when the nights were usually cold. At her car she stopped, keys in hand, and looked up at him.

"I appreciate you waiting," she said.

"Safety is my business," he replied with a touch of irony that he hoped would put some emotional distance between them, because he wanted to kiss her.

But he didn't, even though the moment was so obviously right.

She reached up to lightly touch his face with one hand. He didn't move.

"Nick?"

"I, uh, better go," he said.

She stared up at him for a few brief seconds, probably wondering what the hell his problem was. Why he didn't respond.

Finally, she pressed her lips together hard and pushed the unlock button on the keypad. The car beeped and the locks popped up. She opened the door without looking at him, tossed her stuff inside.

If there was trouble in the financial records, he would probably never be able to see her again. He really hated that. Hated being cut off at the knees.

"Eden?"

She hesitated, then glanced over her shoulder. He reached out to gently turn her, take her face between his palms and kiss her lips. More deeply than she'd kissed him. He'd intended it to be a goodbye kind of kiss, but instead it sent heat coursing through his body.

"I like that," Eden said when he raised his head and slowly let his hands fall away from her face. It'd been the kind of kiss two people might share after a casual date, but it hadn't felt casual.

It felt like a promise.

A promise he didn't think he could keep.

"Eden. I shouldn't have done that."

Her eyebrows drew together. "Kiss me? Why not?"

"I'm not in a good situation right now."

She tilted her head. "How so?"

He opened his mouth to speak, then closed it again. There was no explanation he could give.

"You're not married?" she asked with a sudden frown.

"No. Nothing like that."

"Then…is it just me?"

He shook his head. "No, Eden. It's me. All me."

"Well, in that case," she said, cocking her hand on her hip, "there's something you need to know."

"What's that?" he asked cautiously.

She gave a tiny smirk. "I hate mixed signals. If you can't run the bases, then maybe you shouldn't be up at bat."

WHEN EDEN GOT HOME, she poured herself a glass of wine and heartily wished she could call her sister. Unfortunately, it was 4:00 a.m. in Lyon, and Reggie would not appreciate an early morning this-guy-is-driving-me-to-distraction call, so she'd have to make do with wine alone.

But this guy *was* driving her to distraction. She was receiving definite—albeit cautious— I'm-attracted-to-you signals. And then when she responded, he backed off.

Was her guy radar rusty? Was she no longer able to identify the signs of attraction?

Of course she could. But for whatever reason, Nick was stopping the action as soon as it started, and she'd gotten the message loud and clear tonight.

Which meant Eden was done.

SOMETIMES IT PAID to know the shady at heart. One of Nick's favorite pawnshop contacts had software that could analyze photographs of keys and make duplicates. Before, the guy had had to measure all the points and cut the key by hand. It was an involved process. Nick had never used it, but he knew of Benny's talents. Fortunately, Benny never asked questions, because he didn't want anyone asking questions of him. A true practitioner of the golden rule.

At twilight, Nick parked on the street almost a block away from Tremont Catering so he could watch the parking lot. Patty left at seven. Almost an hour later, Eden left. The building stayed dark after that, and even though he knew that Justin came in as late as ten o'clock, Nick took a chance and left his car, walking down the sidewalk until he could ease into the shadows and then duck down the dead-end alley behind the building.

Benny had done well. The key fit and Nick slipped inside. He made his way to the office through the darkness and closed the door before turning on the computer monitors. He sat still, his ears straining for any sound while the computers started up and he bypassed the password on the first one. In a matter of moments he was downloading data, numbly watching the screen, waiting for the process to stop.

After downloading the data from both computers, he removed the memory stick and dropped it in his pocket. Hopefully this was it.

GABE'S COMPUTER WAS ACTING strangely, flashing boxes onto the screen that told him to run a security check and then, when he clicked those boxes, the screen would go blue and the machine froze up. After the third time it'd happened, he knew that either Nick or Lois was going to have to figure out the problem, and until then, he was going to risk using the community computer in the common area. It was after ten and most of the residents, as Lois so politely called them, were sound asleep.

The computer was on, so all he had to do was shake the mouse and then type, with his two gnarly index fingers. *Bonita Tarrington Wells.* Wells being the name of the guy she'd married after giving up on him.

Why was he doing this?

And if he did find her, what in the hell could he say? I was wrong to choose my job over you?

They both knew that. She'd known it back then. He'd taken another ten years to figure it out—ten years that had slipped by just like that.

She should have given him an earful when he'd contacted her right after his mandatory retirement at the age of fifty-five. But she hadn't. She'd told him she was married, to a man who valued human companionship, and then hung up.

So why wasn't he able to let it go?

Maybe because helping Nick was reminding him of all he'd lost through his own stubbornness.

There were plenty of Bonita Wellses—and none of them seemed right—but there was no Bonita Tarrington Wells. Just as there hadn't been every other time he tried. He kept hoping that something might spring up.

The light behind him snapped on, scaring the bejeezus out of him. He twisted so quickly in his char that he almost hurt his back and looked into the face of his Candlewood nemesis. "Lenny. What the hell? Trying to give me another heart attack?"

Lenny sauntered into the room, followed by

Paul, who moved slower because he used a cane. "Couldn't sleep." He cocked his head. "What the hell are you doing here at this hour?"

"I'm using the computer." Gabe hit the button that closed the screen.

He felt stupidly self-conscious and must have looked it because Paul said, "All the porn sites are blocked."

Gabe cursed under his breath. "I'm not looking up porn. My laptop is acting funny and I wanted to do some research."

"Well, research away. We're going to watch the TV."

As if he'd be able to research with those two in here. Gabe shut off the computer in disgust.

"Lois wants us to leave it on," Paul said.

"Then Lois can turn it back on."

"Hey," Lenny said with a big smile before he slowly sat in one of the leather chairs parked in front of the giant television. "Your grandson seems to be doing all right with Eden."

Yeah, he did, much to Gabe's satisfaction. When the van had pulled away after lessons, she'd been standing in the doorway of the kitchen, watching Nick. Waiting for him.

Paul agreed, finally making it to his own chair and freefalling backwards onto the leather cushions with a satisfied grunt. "Lots of long looks. Makes me wish I was young again."

"We're thinking of starting a pool—" Lenny began, but Gabe raised a hand, cutting him off.

"Don't you dare. This is my grandson."

"But…" Lenny's voice trailed away as Gabe gave him a hard look. Gabe turned to go back to his rooms, pausing briefly in the doorway when he heard Lenny mutter to Paul, "What he doesn't know won't hurt him."

Gabe took the high road and continued down the hall.

"NOTHING," MARCUS SAID. "On these computers, anyway. Bank statements all look reasonable. If they're moving any bad money through the business, it's a negligible amount. So why would they bother?"

"But a five-thousand-dollar cake?" Daphne asked with a grimace. "How do you know he didn't charge the clients one price and double it on the books?"

Nick raised his hand. "I called two of the brides. Well, actually one bride, one mother of the bride. Told them I was thinking of hiring Tremont to make my wedding cake. Were they happy? Was it worth the big price he charged? I managed to get both of them to tell me how much they paid, and it jibes with the records Marcus showed me. I did the same with a couple of the big catering events. They were random, but all four were on the money, so to speak."

"Well, I'm ticked." Daphne wadded up her napkin.

"It was a long shot," Nick said. He couldn't say he was ticked because he was relieved Tremont wasn't involved in a crime, but he was frustrated.

"Hey, we still don't know that Tremont isn't involved," Marcus said, as if looking on the bright side.

"I don't think he is."

"You don't want him to be involved because of his sister," the accountant said pompously.

"I'm a professional," Nick growled. "I like Eden, but I'm not letting that interfere with my work. And who the hell maneuvered things so that we spent time together?"

"I—"

"Threw a rock through a window. Put a note on her windshield. Generally tried to creep her out so she'd seek out a security specialist. Hey, I'm that security guy! How does she know I'm a security guy? Because you told her."

"You did all that?" Daphne asked with a lift of her eyebrows.

"I, uh…" Color started creeping up Marcus's neck. "Maybe."

"I knew it!" Nick said.

"Hey!" Marcus leaned across the table. "We agreed that the end justified the means. My way worked."

"When did we agree on that?" Nick demanded.

Marcus set both palms down on the table in front of him. "It may not have been verbal, but it was damned well understood. I understood it, anyway. All that stuff about unofficial investigations and manning up…"

"If we'd gone through the proper channels, it would never have flown," Daphne agreed. "And now we know. The big question is, do we question Tremont?"

"I don't see what it would get us," Nick mused.

"Or you don't want to see what it gets us?" Daphne asked.

"Just…hold off a bit," he said. "Let me clear up some loose ends."

"Somebody killed Cully," his partner reminded him stiffly.

"It wasn't Justin Tremont," Nick snapped back. "And I really doubt if he knows who did."

"But he might have heard something."

"Agreed." Nick picked up the memory sticks Marcus had left in the middle of the table.

"You don't have to talk to him," Daphne said, seeming to understand his hesitation. "You don't even need to be involved."

Nick nodded. "Just give me a day or two. Let me tie up those loose ends and then we'll decide how to proceed. Okay?"

An impatient look flashed across Daphne's face, but after a quick glance over at an unusually silent Marcus, she said, "Fine.

CHAPTER TEN

NICK WAS DAMNED glad he was able to put Daphne off immediately questioning Justin, because he wanted time to set things right with Eden. He just wished he knew how in the hell to do that.

The obvious way was to tell the truth. He was a cop. They were looking into drug trafficking. Her brother worked in the kitchen and…Nick was investigating them. Unofficially, yes, but if he found anything, he would see that the matter was dealt with in an official capacity.

He'd broken into their files.

Couldn't do it.

He'd tell her he was a cop. The rest would stay buried. Only he, Daphne and Marcus knew.

The Firebird was the only car in the Tremont lot when Nick drove by, so he turned around and headed to Eden's house. The little red Honda was parked on the street under the elm tree. Eden was home for once.

What now?

He got out of the car without a clear plan in mind. If nothing else, he would apologize for the other night, but he hoped she'd give him a chance to…well, he didn't know. He'd been out of the relationship game for so long he wasn't certain what his next step should be.

He rang the bell, then waited on the porch for almost a full minute before Eden opened the door, her expression guarded. "Nick. What a surprise. Service call?"

Great. Sarcasm. "I wanted to talk. Explain about the other night."

"There's something to explain?" she asked coolly.

"Yeah. Like why I said I shouldn't kiss you."

The color rose in her cheeks, staining them pink. "I'm not stupid, Nick. When someone doesn't want to kiss you, it's because they aren't interested."

"No."

"No?" Her eyebrows went up.

He hooked a thumb in his pocket, shifting his weight. "May I come in?"

"What do you mean by 'no'?"

"I mean that I'm interested, but like I said, there are…were…circumstances involved."

"What kind of circumstances?" She continued

to hold her ground, blocking the door, with her head tilted up so she could meet his eyes. Read him.

"Can I come in?" he repeated.

She stepped back. Nick walked into the small living room and she shut the door behind him. "What kind of circumstances?"

"I'm a cop."

She blinked at him. "I thought you were no longer active. I called Reno PD and that's what they told me."

So she'd checked. Good for her. "Because I was suspended. I start back to work on Monday. My lieutenant and I do not see eye to eye and, well, I did something stupid and gave him grounds for an insubordination charge." Followed conveniently by two citizens reporting that he was driving too fast in his cruiser without cause. He'd bet money those people were related to Lieutenant Davidson. "He took advantage of that to teach me a lesson."

"Did you learn anything?" Eden asked.

"Yeah. Not to screw with a new lieutenant."

"What about the security business?"

That was the tough one. Nick had never really lied to someone he cared about before, but the things he'd done, such as hacking into her computers, were part of an investigation. An unofficial yet ongoing investigation. Telling her wasn't going to help anyone, and might well hurt people at some point in time. It was a part of the past he needed to bury so he could move on. Start from square one and see if he could build something.

"An experiment," he finally said.

"In case you became permanently suspended?"

He nodded. "In this economy, my job in law enforcement isn't the most stable."

Eden leaned her head against the door. "I guess that explains the chisel incident," she finally said with a half smile, and Nick felt a glimmer of hope.

He was now at the end of the secrets, the lies and the half lies. Everything from here on would be nothing but the truth. A new start. He could live with the secrets he needed to keep. He hoped.

"It was my first time with a chisel."

"I couldn't tell," she said, gesturing to the kitchen. "I was just making coffee. Want some?" She was still subdued, but not angry. Or as angry.

"Yeah, but there's something else."

"What's that?" she asked with a slight frown, as if she'd suspected there was a catch.

"This." He stepped closer and leaned down to touch her lips with his, the way she'd done to him the other night. He felt her quick intake of breath, and slowly threaded his fingers through her silky hair as he deepened the kiss. But he didn't pull her against him. He wanted her to be able to step back without feeling trapped.

Eden did not take that opportunity. Instead she brought her hands up to capture his face, her warm palms heating his cheeks as they continued to kiss.

"Is that a clear signal?" he asked when he finally raised his head.

"The clearest," she said, touching her fingertips to her lips. "Still want coffee?"

"Yeah," he said, thinking it might be wise to occupy his hands and mouth for the time being, because right now all he wanted to do was haul Eden off to that small bedroom of hers and make love to her in at least a dozen different ways.

He waited until he was sitting at her table and Eden was pouring coffee, giving him the same mug he'd had the last time he'd been there, under much different circumstances. "There's something else you should know."

Her back muscles tensed before she turned to face him. "You really are married?" she said lightly.

Close. "I *was* married."

Eden crossed her arms, closing herself off. "Divorced?"

He shook his head. "I lost my wife two and a half years ago."

She lowered her hands. "I'm sorry."

"Yeah." He had yet to touch his coffee. Didn't know if he would. "What we had…it was good." Eden didn't move, almost as if she was afraid of spooking him or something if she did. "I'm over the bad part. Have been for about a year."

She nodded.

"But I haven't really let anyone back into my life—stuff like dating. I just threw myself into my work."

"Sounds…lonely."

"I have Daphne."

Again Eden's eyes narrowed and he could see she was wondering if Daphne was a dog? A cat? A girlfriend?

"She's my partner. We talked through a lot of issues."

Another nod, and he noticed that Eden had yet to take a drink of her own coffee.

"I'm only telling you this so that maybe you can understand some of my hesitation." Not all of his hesitation, but some of it. "Not to get sympathy or anything." He hated sympathy.

"I understand. I lost my mom. It was a long time ago, but...I still remember. It gets better. Kind of."

He glanced down at the coffee cup, felt the seconds tick past as he debated what to say next, now that he'd dropped the elephant into the room.

"Hey, Nick?" He glanced up as Eden crossed the room toward him. Coming around behind him, she lightly rested her hands on his shoulders. He reached up to cover her fingers with his own, taking in a deep breath that was edged with the light citrus scent of her perfume. "You want to go to a ball game?"

He gave a short laugh. "Baseball?"

"Seems like a good way to break tension, and I have tickets."

He leaned his head back against her and rolled his eyes up to see her face. "I'd love to go to a ball game."

She stepped away and Nick got up from his chair. "What time does it start?"

"Six."

He must have caught her just before she left. "Then we should probably get going." He stood looking down at her.

"Yes." She didn't move.

"Are we going to the game?" he finally asked.

"Yes." But instead of making a move toward the door, Eden closed the distance between them and took his face in her hands to pull his mouth down to hers. He didn't fight her. Instead he wrapped his arms around her and kissed her hard.

When they broke away from each other, they were both breathing hard. "According to the stats I read, it won't be much of a game," Eden said, reaching up to unbutton his shirt.

He grabbed a handful of fabric from behind him, pulling the shirt over his head and dropping it on the floor. Eden took the hem of her long purple T-shirt and did the same. Nick drew her close again and a small tremor went through her as their bare skin touched. He bent his head to kiss her breasts where they spilled out of her demi-bra, and she sucked air between her teeth. She pushed the straps off her shoulders just before Nick impatiently grabbed the edge of the lace and freed her breasts. Her body went hot and liquid as he teased a nipple before pulling it into his mouth.

EDEN HEARD A MOAN and realized it was her own. A low primal sound, unlike any she could ever remember making. Nick undid the bra and tossed it aside. She stepped back to work on the fastening to her jeans, somehow getting it open and the denim, along with her panties, pushed down to the floor. He did the same and she swallowed when she saw his erection. Nice. Very nice.

The next thing she knew he was backing her down the hall toward the bedroom, kissing her as they went. His hard-on pushed against her belly, his hands cupping her ass.

"This will not be slow," Nick muttered as he lowered her onto the bed. "But—" he kissed her lips "—I promise I'll make up for it later."

"Been a while?" Eden asked.

"A long while," he said as he nudged her legs apart. As soon as he pushed into her, her body convulsed and she knew it wasn't going to matter if he was fast, because she was so close to coming. He started moving in her, hard and deep, with that edge of desperation that came from going too long without sex. But even so, it was her body that tensed and then broke into deep throbs of pleasure, which drove Nick even harder. Seconds later he came, too, shooting deep within her before he slowly lowered his damp body on top of hers.

Eden brought a hand up to rest lightly on his

back, soothing the muscles, then traveling up to his neck.

"You okay?" he asked.

"Uh…yeah. I'm okay."

He rolled off her then, flopping onto his back and closing his eyes. Eden laid her head on the pillow and studied his face. He had a great profile and she'd like to see it on her pillow more often.

She wondered if that was going to happen.

He looked over at her. "You want to try to make the game?"

She smiled at him. "I don't know if I can walk…but it is a double header."

A slow smile creased his cheeks. He looked so different when he relaxed. "I didn't come over here to do this, you know."

"Regrets?" she asked lightly.

He took her hand and held it in the center of his chest. "Hardly. I just wanted you to know that my intentions were honorable when I arrived."

"And still are, I imagine."

"Mmm." His eyes shut as he went into man mode. Eden was a fan of man mode because she liked to sleep after sex. But she wasn't ready to sleep yet. Not when this was so new and there were so many facets to explore.

"How'd you get the scar?" she asked quietly,

touching the tip of her finger to Nick's temple. The room was growing darker as the sunlight on the other side of the blind faded, but she could see the long scar that traced over his forehead, just below his hairline.

"Bullet wound," he said, without opening his eyes.

She lightly smacked his shoulder. "Right."

This time his eyes did come open and he rolled onto his side to face her. "Actually, I was knocked off my bike by a car when I was a kid. By a neighbor who was driving while high."

"That's awful." Eden tucked her hand back under the blanket. "I really hate intoxicated drivers."

"Yeah?" he asked gently.

She nodded, meeting his eyes. "My mom was killed by one when I was twelve. Hit-and-run."

"Sorry to hear that."

"It was rough," she said honestly. "Reggie and Justin and me...that's probably why we're so close. We propped each other up." She sensed that Nick was going to ask about her father, and she didn't want to talk about him, so she said, "Do you have brothers or sisters?"

"Not a one."

"You're an only child?"

"I think I was more than enough for my parents. They were pretty busy with their jobs, so I wouldn't have minded a brother or sister."

"What do they do?"

"Mom is the assistant administrator of a hospital in Las Vegas. Dad was a pilot. He retired just last year. As you know," he said with an ironic smile, "I have a grandfather here in Reno."

"My dad left us shortly after my mom died," Eden said bitterly. She had to say something about her father and she may as well get it over with now.

"Wow."

"Long-haul trucker. He hung around for about a year, doing local jobs after she died, but…he ended up back on the road, and Reggie and Justin and I pretty much raised ourselves."

"Is he still alive? Your father?"

"I don't know," Eden said stiffly. "He and Reggie had this big fight and he left, and we never heard from him again."

"You okay with that?"

"It took away a lot of stress." She rolled over to look at Nick. "He used to promise he'd do stuff, and he wouldn't. That he'd be back for this or that important occasion, and he never was. It hurt being lied to all the time. He did it to make life easier for him. We were just kids, but all he thought about was himself."

Nick caressed her face with the back of his hand, smoothing his knuckles down her jawline. She leaned into him. She wanted to ask about his wife, but didn't. If they shared more intimate moments, it might happen, but right now, did it really matter? Did anything matter beyond this particular time they had together?

No. But she truly hoped there'd be other times. She was teetering on the edge of falling for this guy—if she hadn't already done so.

She'd think about that later.

Nick reached out and pulled her close, molding her body against his and stroking his hand up and down her back in a soothing motion. Eden shut her eyes, thinking she'd open them in a minute, when he stopped. But he didn't stop and she drifted asleep in his arms.

She woke to a soft caress traveling down the curve of her spine, and opened her eyes to see that it was dark outside. Pushing herself up on one elbow, she glanced over her shoulder at the clock. Ten. Wouldn't be making the second game of the double header, either. Nick's arms closed around her and she settled into his embrace, stretching out so that they had contact down the entire length of their bodies.

"This is good," he murmured against her hair. The simple phrase warmed her.

Nick took her hand in his, kissed her fingers, then guided them back down where he so obviously wanted them. His eyes drifted shut in a most satisfying way when she took hold of him.

Eden shifted her position so that she was on top of him, holding his gaze as she slowly and deliberately eased him inside her. Then she squeezed her muscles and he groaned, taking hold of her hips, lifting her a few inches and then settling her back on him again. Eden lasted for only a few minutes, Nick much longer; long enough, in fact, that she came again, sucking in a gasp of surprise as her body started contracting once more. He pulled her mouth down to his as he came, throbbing deep inside her.

Eden collapsed on his chest, quite happy to stay there for a decade or so. From the way Nick was smiling, she assumed he was of the same mind.

REGGIE WAS HAVING the time of her life in Lyon, but called at least twice a week to make certain there had been no catering-related catastrophes in her absence—as if Eden would tell her—or any other disasters.

"Glad to hear everything is going well,"

Reggie said after Eden filled her in on the latest bookings and events.

More than well. Eden wanted to tell her sister that she'd started the most amazing relationship. One where the sex was slow and caring. No showmanship.

No games. No other women.

Just a man loving a woman. Happy to give, happy to receive. Plus Nick laughed. With Ian, sex had been so serious. Like an Olympic event, where she was supposed to give him a ten after each performance. And she hadn't realized how much that had bothered her until she'd started sleeping with Nick.

She'd loved to have shared all that, but wasn't going to discuss it with Reggie until Eden knew where this thing with Nick was going. It could be a flash in the pan. A quick flare of passion that would soon burn itself out, and if that was the case, then no one needed to know.

But it didn't feel like that. She'd known him for only a matter of weeks, but Eden felt so right with him. A connection she'd never felt before. It was enough to make her believe that The One actually existed. And that she might have found him.

Eden could hear Rosemary cooing. She must

be snuggled up on her mother's shoulder. "I have news," Reggie said with a note of satisfaction.

You're pregnant. "What?" Eden asked brightly.

"Rosemary is going to have a little brother or sister."

"You're kidding!"

"Nope…and Tom told me you know."

Eden laughed. "I knew before you did."

"I doubt that, but you were right. And we're really happy."

NICK'S FIRST DAY back on the job was jammed-ass busy, to the point that he skipped lunch. Paperwork. He hated paperwork, but it felt good not to be kicking around, trying to figure out how to fill his days. He and the lieutenant had made a tentative peace, which involved a mandatory HR meeting, and Nick had refrained from bringing up the Summit case.

Daphne collared him in the hall right after he got off his shift.

"Did you behave yourself on your first day back?" she asked wryly. At the moment they were working solo while Daphne finished up cases she'd developed during Nick's suspension, and Nick was being flogged with paperwork.

"On my best behavior," he said, wondering what time Eden got off that night. She'd said she had to play it by ear, depending on how the prep went for a luncheon she was catering the next day. They hadn't made any plans or promises, but he wanted to see her again. Soon.

Daphne waited until they were out in the parking lot before she stopped walking. "I talked to the lieutenant about the Summit. Brought up Cully." She kicked the toe of her running shoe into the pavement. "The thing is, without any additional information, he can't okay the man hours on a stalled-out investigation."

"Yeah?" Nick knew what was coming.

"Talk to Tremont, would you? Feel him out. See if he knows anything. Nothing official. Just guy talk."

"Guy talk with a cop."

"Who's sleeping with his sister," Daphne added, as if that would help matters.

"How did you... Nevermind."

"Come on, Nick. Do it."

A bad feeling rolled over him. He shook his head. "I don't want to involve him."

Daphne scowled. "It isn't like I want him to become a CI—"

"Good thing, considering what happened to our last two informants."

"I want some names. I want a starting point."

"If the small fry you bust can't name names, what makes you think Tremont can?"

"I don't know that he can, but I think we can talk to him without him blabbing all over the place." Her lips curled into a smirk. "And we can ask him to keep his ears open, and he might do it."

"Why?"

"Circumstances."

Nick and Eden. "Look, Daph...give me a little time to figure the best way to go at this."

"Fine." She slung the long strap of her purse over her shoulder with so much force that it made a slapping sound when it hit her back. "Guess I'll go see if I can find a meth house."

"Something's wrong," Lenny said on a note of satisfaction.

"Lower your damned voice," Gabe muttered, not looking at Lenny. They were eating breakfast they'd made during the lesson, but the old coot kept staring at first Eden and then Nick. Paul was scowling down at his plate of waffles, making Gabe believe that his bet in the Nick/Eden pool—which had become a reality despite Gabe's protests—was a losing one.

"They're not making any eye contact at all," Lenny announced in a slightly lower voice, which still reverberated through the room. Neither Nick nor Eden seemed to notice.

"Save it," Paul said in a deadly voice.

At the exact same time Gabe said, "Shut up, Lenny."

Lenny blinked at the two men. "I'm just saying…" Then clapped his mouth shut and reached for the syrup.

Gabe shoved a forkful of French toast into his mouth and chewed without tasting it. Lenny was right. There was something off between Nick and Eden. And here he'd had high hopes that even if it didn't develop into anything lasting, at least Nick might get back into the game.

So what now?

EDEN IGNORED NICK for most of the cooking lesson that week. They hadn't managed to get together on Monday and Tuesday, due to him having to put in overtime, but tonight had possibilities. And she didn't want to telegraph that to her elderly students, who were watching the two of them like a flock of geriatric hawks.

They made French toast, pancakes and waffles, and then everyone sat down to a breakfast-for-dinner feast at the table in the rear of the kitchen. By the time the guys piled into the van, Eden was ready for the night to be over.

It had been an exhausting day. She'd had to deal with a complaint about the amount of food served at a luncheon, a bride who insisted on getting the best of the best without paying the price, and Tina Ballard, who had once again changed the menu for the surprise birthday party, as well as the number of guests.

Eden had worked for the Ballards for almost four years and was accustomed to Tina's flighty ways, but she had to insist that this change be the last. If she didn't order the correct amount and type of food, then she couldn't guarantee satisfaction. Tina, however, had been fully cooperative and understanding when Eden had had to explain the hard facts of life. Which was why, despite the woman's case of rampant indecisiveness, she enjoyed working for her.

Ignoring Nick had taken its toll, as well, making Eden edgy as she waited impatiently for the class she usually enjoyed to end. Of course, tonight the guys didn't take their food home with them. They'd eaten it during class. Which had taken forever. She'd gotten a kick out of watching them slowly devour the French toast, waffles and pancakes, but she couldn't help but think that she and Nick could have put the whipping cream and syrup to better use.

He waited in his car until the van left, then followed her home, parking across the street. He caught up with her before she reached the porch, took her tote and the two cookbooks she'd lugged home for research, while she dug out her key.

Once they were inside, he set the books on the end table closest to him, dropped the tote on the sofa and hauled her against him for a real kiss. A soul-searing kind of kiss.

"I need to disarm the system," she murmured against his lips, before putting a hand on his chest.

"By all means," he said, taking off his coat and locking the front door.

When Eden came back into the living room, he kissed her again, then scooped her up in his arms and carried her into the bedroom. She snapped off lights as he walked past them, since she might not be leaving her bed for a while.

Nick undressed her without speaking, slowly removing her clothing, caressing her body with first his fingers and then his lips. It was the first time Eden had ever experienced anything close to worshipping-her-body sex. Once she was naked, he took off his own clothes and then gently laid her on the sheets.

He started at her feet, nuzzling, stroking, and worked his way ever so slowly up her legs until he got up to her most sensitive spot. And then he did what Eden loved most, caressing her breasts and stroking her skin until she bucked against his mouth. Seconds later he entered her, moving slowly, lovingly, until she was on the brink again. He reached down to touch her, once again sending her plummeting over the edge before he, too, came.

"I don't suppose we can do this again tonight?" she asked as she idly stroked his hair.

He rolled off her and lay with his head resting on his arm, the planes and hollows of his handsome face dimly lit by the night-light next to Eden's bed. "I might need a minute," he said with a slow, sexy smile.

"Take your time."

"What's your schedule like next week?"

"Busier than I'd hoped. Justin has one more week of extra shifts at the Lake."

"You don't have to make a cake for him or anything?"

"As if he'd let me," Eden said with a sputter. "That's Patty's territory."

"The Candlewood Center is putting on an event—a poker casino night—and it's a big deal to the guys. Family comes and it's a good time."

Eden propped herself up on her elbows, touched that he would want to invite her. "When?"

"Tuesday the fifteenth. They don't have it on weekends because most people have other plans that don't involve hanging out at an old folks center."

Her face fell. "I'm catering a surprise birthday party. It's for one of the families I cook for. I truly hate surprise parties, but the Ballards have been good to me."

"Trust me. I understand. The guys would have been in seventh heaven to see us together, though."

"Sorry," she said as she stretched out on his firm body, loving the feel of hard muscle beneath her. "Oddly, my line of work can make it very difficult to attend other social functions."

"I can see that." Nick cupped a hand behind her head and pulled her forward for a soft kiss. "You make me feel alive again, Eden. More than I have in a long time."

She smiled, not certain how to respond. Finally, she simply kissed him back, thinking that actions spoke louder than words.

CHAPTER ELEVEN

EDEN AND PATTY served a brunch to a ladies' club on Tuesday morning, arriving back at the kitchen to find Justin sitting on one of the counters, holding a beer and staring into space.

"What's wrong?" Eden asked as soon as Patty had gone into the walk-in with a container of leftovers.

"I just had the most weird-ass experience."

"How so?" Weird-ass experiences were kind of a way of life with her brother.

Justin got off the counter and gestured toward his room with his head. Once there, he closed the door. Eden had a very bad feeling about this, since he rarely felt the need to close Patty, his number one helper, out of his life.

"What?" Eden demanded.

"I was questioned. Unofficially, mind you, by a police officer who wanted information on the kitchen at the lake." He took a card out of his loose pants pocket and flipped it onto the table.

"Detective Daphne," he said with a hint of derision.

Eden drew back slightly when she read the name on the card, then glanced up at her brother, her expression hard. "What kind of goings on?"

"Drug trafficking."

It took her a moment to say incredulously, "They thought *you* were involved?"

"It was damned hard to tell. I didn't get arrested."

Eden moved closer to her brother, stopping directly in front of him, the way she'd done when they were young and she was trying to keep him in line. She folded her arms over her chest. "Is there drug trafficking through the kitchen?"

He shifted the beer from one hand to the other. "It's Lake Tahoe. A *kitchen* in Lake Tahoe."

Oh, great.

People in professional kitchens often worked hard and partied hard, and not always in a legal way. It was part of the culture. And South Lake Tahoe was a party town. But he still hadn't answered her question. After another few moments of silence, he said, "It's common knowledge there's drug traffic through that hotel. Even the cops know."

"Do you know who's involved or how?"

"Not really, because I've made no effort to find out. Kind of a health-and-safety issue, you know? I don't use and I don't ask questions. I make pastry."

"But…don't you have to take a drug test to work there?"

Justin smiled. "Drug tests pick up users, not sellers."

"Wow." Eden leaned back, pushing her hair away from her face with both hands. Then she slanted a sideways look at her brother.

"The job is a good one," he said before she could voice her concern. "There are plenty of nice people there who have nothing to do with the few guys who make connections. I'm one of them." He reached out to pat her hand in a brotherly way. "I'm back to three nights a week as of tomorrow. If I can get another pastry job somewhere else, I will, but for right now, it's a good opportunity, good pay and good connections to potential catering clients."

"I feel very conflicted about this."

"I know," Justin said with a sigh, lifting his beer to his lips. "I know."

Eden hesitated for a moment, then asked her final question on the subject. "Do you know anything that might help the police get a handle on the situation?"

"Nothing the police themselves don't already know. Nothing that would further an investigation."

Enough said. For now. But Eden had a lot she was going to say to Nick whenever she saw him next.

She didn't have to wait long. Justin had taken off for his job at the lake, which made her feel a bit sick, knowing what she did now. She was closing up the kitchen for the night, having shooed Patty home, when Nick's SUV pulled into the lot. Her stomach tightened. Showtime.

He came into the kitchen with that open smile that would have melted her heart a few hours ago. When he saw the expression on her face, he stopped a few feet away form her. "What?"

"Didn't you once tell me that your partner's name was Daphne?"

"Yes."

"Would that be the same Daphne that just questioned my brother about drug trafficking?" Nick's expression instantly closed off. "How many Daphnes can there be on one police force?" Eden continued, as if asking a rhetorical question.

Nick's face could have been carved from ice when he said, "I imagine it was my partner." *Who was this man?*

Eden shifted her weight, settling a hand on her hip. "Why Justin? Have you found something that makes you think he's involved in drug trafficking?"

"We don't think Justin is involved."

"We?" she asked, her voice rising slightly.

"I am a cop, Eden. On a drug task force."

"Why Justin?" she repeated.

"There's drug traffic connected with some of the people working at the Lake Summit Hotel at Tahoe. Large amounts that are shipped out and smaller amounts sold locally. We were hoping that Justin might have heard or seen something."

Eden tried to moisten her lips, but her mouth was too dry. Pieces were falling into place and she didn't like the picture they formed.

"It was no accident that you came to Tremont for cooking lessons with your grandfather, was it?"

He pulled in a breath, then shook his head. "I'm not going to lie to you. No. No accident."

"You came to spy on Justin."

"Not exactly."

Eden rolled her eyes to the sky, blinking rapidly. "It's going to get worse, isn't it?"

"I came to get a look at your business. See if there was any sign that all was not as it seemed financially."

"I don't—" She looked away abruptly, pressing her lips together.

"Drug money has to be laundered," he stated. "Small businesses are great for that. A catering firm might be one way to pass bad money into the system." She turned back to him. "We know now that's not the case. Tremont has been taken out of the investigation."

"Why?"

"We've received information that indicates your records are clean."

"Damned right they're clean." Eden swallowed, but couldn't tamp down the outrage welling up in her. He'd used her. He'd come to her kitchen with a nefarious purpose in mind and he'd lied to her.

"You know, Nick? It's been a hell of a night." She took a couple steps away from him, then rested one hand on the stainless-steel counter, her fingers gripping the edge. "I need you to go now."

"Eden…"

"Now, Nick. Leave now or I'll call your brothers in blue and ask them to remove you." She smiled grimly. "You wouldn't want to risk another suspension, would you?"

"I didn't sleep with you because I was spying on Justin."

"Was that part of the investigation over?" she asked. "I can see by your face it was."

"I didn't go into this thinking I'd fall for you. I was trying to do my job. I care for you, Eden."

"If that's true—if you honestly care for me—then do me a big fat favor and get out of here."

NICK WAS HOT. He drove straight to Daphne's apartment and pounded on the door. A few seconds later she jerked it open with a belligerent look on her face.

"Did you talk to Justin Tremont?" he asked as evenly as possible.

"Yeah. I questioned Tremont. No stone unturned."

Nick shoved his hand into his hair. "You could have warned me. Given me some time to…set the stage."

"Set the stage for what, Nick?"

"You knew I was seeing Eden."

"Yeah? So?"

"Well, she figured out who you are. And why I must have been at the kitchen."

"How in the hell did she do that?"

"Because I mentioned your name once, I guess. As my partner."

"That was your mistake." Daphne turned and walked into her apartment.

Nick followed. He never ceased to be amazed at how much her place was at odds with her personality, given all the soft draped fabrics and colors. The Sig .45 sitting on a towel on the coffee table, where she'd obviously been cleaning it, seemed wildly out of place. Unless you knew Daphne.

"Does she know you stole her computer files?"

"No. And I would very much appreciate it if you didn't tell her that." He still had that secret, was still lying by omission.

Daphne cocked her head. "Look, Nick. I'm sorry if I screwed up your love life. Frankly, I was glad you were finally developing one, although I probably wouldn't have chosen the sister of a suspect as my dream date."

"Former suspect."

"Right." She put a hand on her hip, rustling the blue silk robe she wore. Marcus would have had his tongue on the floor if he could have seen her. "But someone killed my CI and fed me bad information, and I want a resolution."

"Our CI," Nick said. "And I want to get to the bottom of it, too."

"I'm sorry about your love life," Daphne said again, in a way that made him wonder, and not for the first time, if she had ever been in love.

Nick's mouth tightened. "I've got to go."

Daphne opened the door for him and he stepped out into the carpeted hallway. And because he was still so pissed, he didn't say anything to make the situation between them better.

EDEN'S SHEETS SMELLED like Nick, so she stripped them off the mattress and tossed them into a corner. It was too late to do laundry, so she hauled her extra blankets out of the linen closet and went to bed on the sofa. And once she was settled there in her living room, she stared up at the dark ceiling with eyes that were puffy from crying and threatening to produce tears again.

She'd thought Ian was a liar. Ha! He was bush league compared to Nick. Sneaking around, spying on her and her family.

She pressed a hand against her eyes as tears started to seep out the corners. Played for a fool. In the worst way.

And this time it hurt so badly.

She flopped over on her side, drawing the covers around her tightly. She missed her sister. She so needed to talk to her, but wasn't going to dump this mess in Reggie's lap.

No. She was going to dump it in Justin's, since he was the one involved.

The next morning she caught him at the kitchen and asked him to stop by her place that afternoon before he took off for the lake. When he showed up, just after she'd returned home from a client consultation and had kicked off her heels, she hauled him in, pressed a cold beer into his hands and told him exactly what she'd learned about Nick.

"Let me get this straight," Justin said as he popped open the beer and dropped the top in the bamboo trash can next to Eden's kitchen sink. "*Nick* was investigating *us* for money laundering. It wasn't just this Detective Daphne chick."

"Isn't that what I just said?" Eden asked irritably.

"I wanted to make certain that was what I heard. Shit." Justin took a long swallow of beer. "He thought *I* was laundering money."

"Yes."

"Which must have meant that he thought I was selling drugs."

"Probably. Or taking care of the money for someone who was."

"Well, that kind of pisses me off," he said in a deceptively light voice as he sat in a chair across the table from her.

Eden gave her brother a weary look, but could see that he was very, very angry. Justin had never been one to explode. No. He did more of a slow burn, hiding both anxiety and pain behind a flippant front. As he was doing now.

"Why did he decide we weren't laundering money?"

"I don't know. I don't know how these things work. He just said they got information that indicated we were in the clear." *And that he could sleep with me.*

"I think bank records require a subpoena or warrant."

"I couldn't tell you what happened. Just that I feel used." Eden pressed a palm to her forehead. "Really used."

"And this happened before you two…" Justin let his voice trail off.

Eden was shocked. "How'd you know about us?"

He gave her a pained look. "The old guys

gossip about you. I could hear them in my room, because most of them speak at very high decibel levels." He drew his eyebrows together in a frown, one hand still on his forgotten beer. "I'm pissed," he repeated.

Eden knew the feeling.

REGGIE WAS DUE back in two weeks and Eden was determined the business would be running smoothly when she arrived—even though Eden was having one hell of a time concentrating. Every now and then tears of anger, and regret, would swell, and she had to hide them from the ever vigilant Patty.

Wedding season would be starting soon, and with it an upsurge in bookings. Eden would be too busy to think. But right now she had time and hated it.

She was so damned mad at Nick, felt so damned used.

What really killed her was that she'd been well on the way to falling in love with the guy she'd thought he was. Hell, she was in love with that guy.

On top of the Nick trauma, she couldn't say she was thrilled about Justin's job at the lake anymore, either. It was a fact that some casino hotels had a dark element to them. The owners and operators worked hard to keep their businesses on the up and up, but with such huge staffs, they couldn't control everything. In fact, Eden had come to realize on one of her many sleepless nights that the setting was incidental. It could have been at a ski lodge or a bus garage or a T-shirt shop.

But it wasn't. The place the police were investigating was the hotel where her brother worked, and it worried her.

She couldn't blame Nick for that.

"IT DIDN'T WORK out," Lenny said, shouting across the poker table. "You and Eden? It didn't work out?"

"No." Nick cut his grandfather a look, but Gabe kept his eyes on his cards. Apparently everyone was disappointed in Nick for screwing up with Eden. He couldn't very well tell them the truth, that the relationship was doomed from the start because of what he'd had to do, so he kept his mouth shut.

But he was going to do something, because the situation was eating at him. He figured he'd give her some time to be totally torqued off at him, then he'd work on damage control. He had to, because he was pretty certain he was in love with her.

"She canceled next week's lesson, you know." Paul glared at Nick.

"I don't think it was because of me." He tossed a couple cards on the table. "I'll take two." Lenny dealt him two, off the top of the deck this time.

"Where's that Marcus kid?" Lenny asked, looking around as if he'd find him behind a potted plant. "He's supposed to be here tonight."

"No idea," Nick said. He avoided Marcus at work. And he couldn't say things were grand between him and Daphne. She was hell-bent on cracking the drug ring, and seemed to think he was a slacker because he'd objected to her methods.

She wasn't wrong in questioning Justin…Nick just wished he'd had some warning she was going to do it.

"Nick's taking me shopping tomorrow," Gabe commented as he threw some cards down. "Three."

"I need pancake mix," Paul said.

"Tomato sauce and onions," James added.

"We'll make lists after the game," Nick promised.

He drew a deep, silent breath, feeling as if

he'd been run over by a truck. Who would have thought cooking lessons would have such a devastating effect on his life?

THE GAME HAD gone on forever and the entire time Nick had sat staring at his cards or the table with a deep frown. Lenny kept making wisecracks and every now and then he'd say something about cooking class, then glance over at Nick, who ignored him. Gabe had wanted to pop him one.

"Would you mind telling me what that was all about?" Nick asked as soon as he and Gabe left the common area. "All that stuff about things not working out with Eden?"

"Just Lenny flapping his lips," Gabe said in a clipped voice. "Lenny's an idiot, and these guys gossip about everything."

It was obvious to Gabe that Nick wasn't buying it, even if it was the truth. He stopped in the center of the hall.

"I know you're trying to help," he said, "but you gotta quit trying to set me up. I can handle my own life, Granddad."

"But are you?"

"What does that mean?" Nick hooked a thumb in his front pocket, his chin slightly jutted out in a way that reminded Gabe of himself back in the day.

"Years slide by, Nick. They evaporate. One minute you're thirty-five and deep in the job. The next thing you know you're fifty-five, facing mandatory retirement and you've become a closed-off son of a bitch who no one wants anything to do with. Then you're seventy and—" He broke off abruptly.

Nick stared at him. "You want to flesh that out a little?"

Gabe closed his eyes. No, he didn't. But maybe if he did, then Nick would understand a few things. About him, and about life.

"Let's go to my rooms."

GABE'S STORY WAS pretty lean and Nick had had to fight to get some actual details out of him. After Gabe's wife had left, he'd been devastated, but too macho to let it show. Instead he dove into his work, let that define his life. He met a woman— Bonita Tarrington—who'd put up with him for longer than he deserved. She finally drew a line in the sand, demanded that he either cut back his workload and pay attention to her or she was leaving.

"I let her go," Gabe said. "Work was safe.

Wouldn't divorce me or die on me or anything. Stupid move. I tried to go out with other women, but it didn't feel the same."

For a long moment Nick simply stared at his granddad. He'd never had a clue that any of this had happened. Gabe had always seemed so happy being single and alone. "Have you tried to find her?"

Gabe's shoulders slumped before he said, "I called her after I retired. She basically told me to go to hell."

"But you still think about her."

"Yeah. I…made one hell of a mistake letting her go."

"Find her," Nick said. "The worst she could do is tell you to go to hell again."

"I've been trying," Gabe practically shouted, his pale eyes blazing. "Now that I'm a shriveled-up old fart, I'm trying to find her. Maybe she's dead. Maybe she has dementia. Maybe she's still happily married."

Okay. This was a touchy subject and Nick needed to tread lightly. "How long ago did you last contact her?"

"Over twenty years." Gabe studied the floor. Very uncharacteristic for him, a man who usually met life head-on. "I understand there are no guarantees, and even if Bonita and I had made a life when I'd tried to contact her, it may not have worked. But I also understand that had I not been so short-sighted, I may have had companionship through some of my lonely years."

The pieces clicked into place. "And that's what you want for me."

Gabe made a frustrated gesture. "I can see you heading down the same path I did, if that's what you mean. Don't do it. Things didn't work out with Eden, but it's a start. Try again. Find someone to share your life, even if it's only a couple of years or weeks or even days. Because life passes faster than you ever dream." Gabe shot him a quick look. "But I like Eden. Any chance…?"

Nick shook his head then focused on the coffee table.

A very long silence followed and then he heard his granddad exhale. Two stubborn men at an impasse. Finally he raised his head. "You want me to see if I can find Bonita?"

Gabe stiffened. "It wouldn't involve anything unethical, would it?"

"Like using the police databases? No." Nick had pushed that particular envelope and had lived to regret it. "But Marcus is good with this kind

of stuff. I can ask him to see if he can find her."
It might be a way for them to start talking again.

It took his granddad a long time to answer, but
finally he nodded. "Unless you don't think it's
wise," Nick said, not wanting to push his granddad into anything.

"No. I want to find her." Gabe spoke without
emotion.

After another long silence, Nick said, "Scared?"

"Like a little girl."

EDEN HAD JUST finished the book work for the
day and was about to leave the kitchen when the
office phone rang. It was after normal business
hours and she almost let it keep ringing, which
spoke volumes about her current mood. Eden
never let an opportunity pass. But now she didn't
particularly care if this was opportunity calling.
She was having one hell of a time going back to
living the way she had before Nick came barg-
ing in, upsetting her equilibrium and destroying
what little trust Ian had left intact.

After the fourth ring, she couldn't take it any
longer and answered. "Tremont Catering."

"Eden? This is Lois at the Candlewood Center."

Eden's stomach lurched. *What now?* "Hi,
Lois."

"I called, well, for clarification really. The guys are enjoying your class and, while I understand that you had to cancel this week's class, I need to know…are you going to continue to give the classes?"

"I…" *Had hoped to have a few days to figure that out.* Right now she was still recovering from an emotional blindside.

"If you can't, which I fully understand," Lois said in a way that told Eden she'd heard the same gossip about her and Nick that Justin had, "then I want to make alternative arrangements."

Eden hesitated, reluctant to commit, because being around Gabe would only remind her of Nick. And it wasn't as if she could tell Lois, "Yes, I'll give the class, but don't bring Gabe."

"Can I get back to you?" Eden finally asked. "I need to firm up a few things."

"Certainly." Lois didn't sound happy.

"I'll give you a definite answer soon."

"Thanks, Eden. I hope you continue. The guys loved the class and they're all cooking to some extent now."

"Glad I could help." Even if it had turned her life upside down. It wasn't her class's fault that Nick had used her.

"HERE, LET ME get the door," Nick said as he followed his granddad down the hall to his apartment, which was only slightly larger than Gabe's but had more room in the kitchen.

"You have the groceries," Gabe said, coming to a stop. "And I'm not helpless. Give me your keys."

Nick maneuvered his hand from beneath the bulging paper bag to drop the keys into Gabe's open palm. His granddad unlocked the door and pushed it open, then made his way inside.

"You sure you know what to do with all that stuff?" Gabe asked as Nick dumped the two bags onto his kitchen table, which creaked. They were going to make the stuffed cabbages—his grandfather's favorite dish—at Nick's place while they watched the game. This would be Gabe's offering for the family casino-night potluck.

It'd keep Nick from thinking about Eden and screwing up royally. Lies and more lies. And Cully's murderer was still out there and drugs were still moving through the Tahoe Summit.

Life went on.

"The trick to stuffed cabbage is sour salt," Nick said as he pulled the small jar out of the bag. Nick had done a fair amount of internet research in order to learn the ins and outs of making stuffed cabbage. It wasn't like he could ask Eden about it.

"I see." Gabe gave a slight frown, as if Nick was speaking in a foreign tongue. "And here I thought it was cabbage," he said drily.

"Another important component," he agreed.

He'd just gotten the water boiling to blanch the cabbage leaves when the phone in his inside jacket pocket rang. He dug it out and answered without looking at the number.

"Justin Tremont had a car accident on the Carson Grade." Daphne's voice was subdued. "He's alive," she added, anticipating his first question.

Thank God for that. "When'd it happen?"

"Almost two hours ago. They had to transport him, but he's all right. For the most part." She paused for a second before adding. "I thought you might want to know."

Damn right he wanted to know. And all he could think about was what Eden must be going through right now.

"What hospital?"

"Saint Mary's. And Nick?"

"Yeah?"

"There are some concerns."

Oh, shit. "Can you meet me there?" he asked.

"I'm here now."

"I'll see you in ten," he said, ending the call. He turned to his granddad, who was watching him intently. "I have to go to the hospital."

"Someone I know?" Gabe asked. "A cop?"

"No. Maybe part of a case." He grabbed his keys up off the table. "I don't know how long this is going to take. You want me to take you home? Or stay here."

"Maybe I can come along?"

Nick hesitated only for a moment. "Sure. Come on."

CHAPTER TWELVE

EDEN HAD ALWAYS hated that Firebird as much as Justin loved it. Well, the Firebird was no more, and Justin had come within a hairbreadth of following suit. A seat belt had pretty much saved him after his car had missed a curve coming down the Carson Grade.

Thankfully, although he was on an IV and bandaged up with a broken tibia and a serious concussion, he was pronounced in stable condition. The thing that disturbed her, though, was that when she got the visit from the highway patrol, they'd specifically asked her not to talk to anyone. Not even Reggie, who was going to kill her.

Eden closed her eyes and leaned her head against the wall as she waited for the medical staff to do whatever they had to do before they allowed her back inside her brother's room.

"There she is." Eden's eyes came open at a familiar voice. Gravelly and impatient. Gabe. And, of course, Nick. On the opposite side of Gabe stood a striking dark haired woman with a no-nonsense expression. This couldn't be good in any way, shape or form.

Eden moved in front of Justin's door.

"You're not going in there," she said to no one in particular. In response, the woman took out a badge case and flipped it open. "Daphne Sparks, Washoe-Tahoe Drug Task Force."

So this was Daphne. Eden instantly decided she didn't like her.

"My brother is injured and you're not going in and upsetting him."

"I'm not going in to upset him," Daphne said, looking as if she was seconds away from forcibly moving Eden.

"Right. Because you're not going in."

"Yeah, I am."

"Daph…" Nick said in a warning voice. He shifted his gaze to Eden. "We need to talk to Justin about the circumstances of the accident. We have a witness who suggests that it wasn't an accident. We need corroboration."

"Not an accident?" Eden felt the blood leave her face. "Because of…" she glanced at Daphne "…his job?" Otherwise a highway-patrol investigator would be there, not a drug-task-force member.

"We don't know." Nick spoke in a flat cop voice, but his eyes were far from emotionless. There was a veritable storm going on in their depths. "And we need to talk to Justin to find out."

"I want to be there."

He shook his head. "You can't." His voice took on a gentler note as he said, "We won't be long."

Eden let out a breath before grudgingly stepping aside. Daphne knocked, and when the door opened, she and Nick went inside, leaving Eden out in the hall with Gabe, who shifted uncomfortably.

Before the door had closed all the way, it opened again and the two nurses who'd been in the room came out.

"As soon as they're done, you can go in," the taller nurse said to Eden. Then she and her associate walked down the hall in the opposite direction.

Gabe cleared his throat and Eden glanced at him. He reached out and awkwardly took her hand, holding it in his warm, surprisingly strong grip. "I'm sure sorry this happened," he said.

"Me, too." Eden swallowed, determined to hold it together.

"Nick about went out of his head on the way over here," Gabe added helpfully.

"I see." She looked at the door, then back at the old man. "Your grandson has put me through hell, you know."

"For the record," Gabe stated, "I suspect you've done the same for him."

"Then I guess he got what he deserves," Eden said.

JUSTIN'S FACE AND PART of his head were bandaged. He had tubes in his good arm and his eyes were almost swollen shut. He looked like hell, but he was alive, Nick thought, which was saying something after seeing the photos of the accident scene.

"You," he slurred, looking at Nick through those puffy eyes.

"Yeah, me," Nick said. "Can you remember the accident?"

Justin made a slight up and down movement with his head. "Hit from behind."

Daphne stepped closer to the bed. "Can you remember the vehicle?"

"Jeep Grand Cherokee. Dark." He formed

each word slowly but distinctly, then paused to swallow. "Prob'ly the one with the Hemi, since it caught my Firebird."

"You weren't speeding, were you?" Nick asked with a half smile.

Justin tried to smile back, but failed.

"Do you think the hit was deliberate?"

"Yes." The word was low but adamant.

"Any idea who?" Nick asked.

It took Justin a few seconds to say slowly, "I may know who."

"Who?" Nick repeated quietly, glad that Daph was keeping her mouth shut.

"After we talked," he said to Daphne, "I asked a friend at the lake…a couple questions about drugs. If it was getting…worse." He swallowed drily. "Thought he was like me."

"Clean?" Nick asked. Justin gave a weak nod.

"And someone decided you might be a narc?" Daphne spoke for the first time.

Justin cut a glance toward her. "Narc…money launderer. Many accusations." He almost smiled and then his eyes drifted shut. "I didn't think…"

"It's okay," Daphne said.

"Can you give me your friend's name?" Nick asked.

"Yeah. Ronnie Esparza. Works the evening shift. Salad station."

"Thanks," Daphne said, stepping away from the bed.

Justin's eyes came open again, zeroing in on Nick. "I'm worried about Eden."

"I'll take care of her."

"Good." His eyelids lowered again before he muttered, "Damn, I hurt."

NICK AND DAPHNE came out of the room together, talking in low voices. They conferred for a few seconds after the door to Justin's room closed behind them, then Daphne gave a curt nod and headed toward the exit. She acknowledged Eden with a quick glance and then was gone.

Which left Nick.

Whom Eden didn't particularly want to see.

"I need to talk to you," he said in that same emotionless voice as before. "Will you excuse us, Granddad?" he added when Eden got to her feet.

They walked a few yards away to a potted palm next to an empty desk. Nick's hand came to rest at her elbow, but she shook it off.

"Here's the deal," he said in a low voice, once again taking her upper arm in a loose grip, as if afraid she'd bolt before he was done talking.

"Daphne and I are working on your brother's accident." Eden opened her mouth, but Nick cut her off. "We have a good idea of what's going on and there's an excellent possibility that we'll have a satisfactory resolution."

A satisfactory resolution. What would one of those feel like?

Eden pulled her arm away and hugged herself. "And that's it."

"No." His mouth tightened for a moment. "That's not it. You need to know that everything I did…I had a reason. I had choices to make and I didn't make them lightly. This has cost me, too."

Eden nodded, not meeting his eyes, not wanting to see what was in their depths. Because she was afraid? Hell, yes.

"Justin's worried about your safety."

Her gaze came up then. "I have a state-of-the-art security system," she said coldly. But she didn't feel nearly as brave as she sounded. Someone had forced her brother off the road and now Justin was concerned about her safety.

"Make sure you turn it on," Nick replied with equal coolness. Cop coolness. This was not the Nick who cooked with his grandfather or hit himself in the face with a chisel, or the Nick that had shared her bed. Eden swallowed as she studied his face. This was a man she didn't know. Didn't care to know.

Like Ian, Nick had a second face.

"Thanks for the tip," she said. "Will you keep me updated?"

After her sarcastic comment, she expected more copspeak. Instead, the emotionless mask slipped for a moment as he said, "I want you safe."

Eden felt an odd sensation move through her at his adamant tone, a remnant of that connection she'd yet to totally sever. Perhaps now was the time.

"Here's the deal. My family was fine until you and your partner took it upon yourselves to investigate us. Now we are no longer fine."

"Eden…I am sorry that things got so screwed up. I was doing my job."

"Somehow that doesn't make things any better, does it?"

He glanced back at Gabe, then shifted his weight. "I need to get my granddad to his rooms and then I'm going to meet with Daphne."

"All right." Eden could think of nothing else to say.

"One last thing. We're keeping the circumstances of what happened quiet, hoping that whoever did it won't go to ground, or harass the witness. Any chance the Summit might call you when he doesn't show up to work?"

"No idea, but I'll avoid their calls."

"Thank you." Nick's mouth tightened for a moment, then he turned and walked away, leaving Eden under the fronds of the tall potted palm. She stayed there, watching him walk beside Gabe down the hall toward the exit. Then she drew in a shaky breath and headed to her brother's room—only to find him sound asleep.

And perhaps, in her current state of mind, that was a good thing. She needed some time alone to work up the anger again.

She didn't get that time.

"This isn't his fault," Justin muttered, in such a low voice she could barely make out the words. But she did.

"How can you say that?" she demanded.

Justin's chest rose and fell slowly. "He was doing his job. He had every reason to suspect me. I worked at drug central and I drove a really expensive car."

"He lied to me."

Justin rolled his head to look at her, his expression pinched. "Just think about it for a while, okay? Think about what Nick could and couldn't have done."

Eden rubbed her palms over her face, then sat staring at the wall behind her brother's bed.

"Hell, you think he wanted to fall for you? What with you being all prickly and mean?"

"I am not prickly and mean," Eden said. "And I don't know that he fell for me. I think he used me."

"You do a good imitation of prickly and mean," Justin muttered. "And I've watched the guy around you. He's in deep."

"If he was in deep—"

"Damn. It. Eden. I'm trying to let the drugs take effect."

"Then you should have continued to pretend to be asleep." It felt so incredibly good to be able to yell at Justin that she was doing her best to ignore the stabs inflicted by the topic of conversation.

Justin gazed at her through those puffy eyes. "If he was in deep, what? He would have told you he was investigating us? When? When he first came to the kitchen? On the second visit? Third? What was he supposed to say? 'Oh, by the way, I'm really a cop who faked his way into your life to see if your brother is a criminal, but now I know he's not. Want to make out?'"

Eden stood up because she was too agitated to sit. She hated that what Justin said made sense, because she had sworn to herself that she was never going to tolerate being lied to again. Not in a major way, anyhow. Only in the of-course-that-doesn't-make-your-butt-look-big way. She pushed her hair back, clutching a handful and holding it at the top of her head.

"I think he's a good guy. Trying to do his job."

Eden squeezed her eyes shut. "I don't know, Justin...." Her tone sounded so much like whining that she snapped her mouth shut again.

"That's because there's nothing to know. He was in a lose-lose situation and he still fell for you."

"I—"

"Need to give Nick a break and let your brother get some sleep. We'll talk when I come out of the coma."

Eden sighed and walked over to the bed. "I'm sorry. I didn't mean to..."

"Ruin my day?" he said with a touch of wryness. "No problem. Have this all sorted out before I come to, okay?"

"I'll do my best," Eden said. Just as soon as she sorted a few hundred things out in her brain.

NICK WANTED TO nail the asshole who'd tried to kill Eden's brother, but the Ronnie Esparza lead was not panning out—mainly because he was nowhere to be found. His mother, his girlfriend, his boss—no one seemed to know where to find him which frustrated the hell out of Nick. Esparza's name was being released as a person of interest in an ongoing investigation, but Nick wasn't holding out much hope.

After chasing down his fifth dead-end lead, he finally got through to the one witness they had—the woman who'd called the highway patrol to report the accident. She thought the poor man standing next to his damaged SUV had hit an animal, and didn't know if his vehicle was operational or if he had a phone. When HP went to investigate, they'd found Justin in his totaled Firebird at the bottom of the canyon and no Grand Cherokee.

"I didn't see the accident," the woman told Nick after he'd identified himself and explained the reason for his call. "I came round the corner, saw a very damaged SUV parked beside the road and a man outside it, looking over the edge of the embankment. I started to slow, but he waved me on." She paused and then said, "Being a woman alone at night, well, you understand. So I dialed the highway patrol."

"What kind of SUV was it?"

"Something dark. Maybe a Jeep? Or a Pathfinder? I'm not certain. Its front end was quite smashed up. Like he'd hit a deer or a bear or something. That's why I think he was peering over the embankment. To see what happened to the animal."

"What did he look like? The guy?"

"Umm. Tallish. Thin. His hair was long, blowing back in the wind."

"Age?"

"I couldn't tell you. Not super old."

"All right. Thank you. I hope you don't mind if I call you back if I have any more questions?"

She didn't mind and Nick hung up the phone. Tall, thin guy with longish hair. Not too many of those in the world.

Nick tossed an empty pen across the room and into the trash.

What now?

Marcus came into the room then, carrying a computer printout and, for a brief moment, Nick felt a glimmer of hope. "You got something on the Tremont hit-and-run?"

"No." Marcus laid the sheet on Nick's desk.

"But I did find Bonita Tarrington Wells. She's living in a retirement community outside of Pahrump."

PATTY CAME IN to help on Sunday morning, and Eden went through the familiar motions of making and packing four days of easy-to-reheat gourmet meals into containers.

"Would you like me to deliver?" Patty asked.

"No." She shook her head. Patty did not know what had happened to Justin, and was openly curious about the half-finished cake that was due to be delivered the next day. Eden had already called and offered a full refund, plus a percent off a future cake. The customer wasn't happy, but she didn't think he'd be any more pleased if she tried to decorate it herself.

"I'm more than happy to," Patty persisted.

Eden pushed the hair off her cheek with one hand. "I have to talk to Mrs. Ballard about the party setup." The biggest pain of surprise parties in a home—setting them up without the guest of honor being any the wiser. "But…I guess you could deliver the Stewart meals."

"It's on my way home," Patty said, pleased to be needed.

Eden helped her load the cooler and boxes

into her car, and then packed her own cooler and boxes into her Civic. She was so thankful that March had been slow for them. It hurt the pocket-book, but in other ways was a sanity saver. Eden didn't know if she could fake too many parties. As it was, she and Patty and a temp were doing two luncheons that week, but at least they were buffets and Eden wouldn't have to serve or smile or be on her A game.

At the moment, she didn't know if she could fake a C game. Feeling lied to and betrayed by Nick was bad enough, but now her biggest fear was that whoever had tried to run Justin off the road would try again once they discovered they'd failed.

She was so damned glad she had that alarm system, even if she'd been scammed into getting it. She still hadn't figured out why Nick had... Her fingers tightened on the steering wheel. To get access to her house and her records, of course. How else had he known they were "clean," as he called it?

She made a sharp left turn into the Ballard driveway and headed through the wrought-iron gate.

Calm. Down.

Eden unloaded the cooler as she'd done every

Sunday for the past four years, and dragged it behind her up the flagstone walk to the back entrance. Drop this stuff off, talk to Tina, then head down the hill to check on Justin.

She left the cooler on the patio and returned to her car for the box. When she got back to the patio, the cooler was gone and the back door propped open. Michael Ballard, the birthday boy, appeared and took the box from her.

"Hey, Eden. Good stuff as always?" He was a tall, round man with a fringe of red hair and a penchant for cardigan sweaters when he wasn't wearing a business suit.

"The best," she said, smiling, trying to appear normal. "Is Tina here?"

"She sure is." He winked and said, "I'll just *disappear* while you talk." Eden tilted her head, frowning slightly, when he cupped a hand next to his mouth and whispered, "I know about the *p-a-r-t-y.*"

She firmed her lips in mock disapproval. "Better keep quiet about that."

He laughed. "I'll go to my den and save her the trouble of kicking me out."

Footsteps sounded in the hall and Michael put a finger to his lips and slipped out the back door on the patio. Tina stuck her perfectly coiffed dark head into the kitchen, then looked down the hall. "I thought I heard Michael."

"He helped me bring in the meals, and then went outside."

"Excellent." Her client smiled. "Now, here's the plan. We will leave at six o'clock to visit our married daughter, and hopefully be back at seven. That only gives you an hour. Can you do it?"

"I can do it," Eden said with a show of enthusiasm she hoped didn't sound forced.

"Great. I'll leave the side door open, because Michael never checks that one before we leave." Tina brought her hands together. "This will be so much fun."

"Oh, yes," Eden said. "I can't wait."

Happy people, happy times, while her own life was disintegrating around her.

NICK TOOK A few paces down the gravel road where a sheriff's deputy had found the Jeep Grand Cherokee abandoned in the desert near Virginia City. The front bumper and grille were smashed and telltale streaks of dark blue paint that matched Justin's Firebird radiated down the passenger side of the vehicle.

"There are tire tracks here where someone

turned a vehicle around," the highway patrolman pointed out. "The driver got picked up."

"Yeah," Nick said. He'd wanted to inspect the scene before the rig got hauled off to impound. Not much to see, except for the tire marks from the other vehicle and the blown front tire on the Jeep, which was probably why they'd abandoned it in the open. The plates were gone and the VIN number had been obliterated. But there should still be a number on the engine block, which he hoped to have by the end of the day. That and fingerprints.

They'd had absolutely no luck finding Ronnie Esparza. The guy had quit the country, leaving Nick to wonder if he'd been working alone or under orders. Or if, once his mission had been completed, he'd shared Cully's fate.

RENO PD HAD no extra manpower to speak of, but Nick managed to get a couple patrols down Eden's street, just in case. Justin was still in the hospital and no one had asked any questions about him. No anonymous phone calls looking for updates. Nothing like that.

"Did you sleep last night?" Daphne asked, walking into the office as Nick poured his ump-teenth cup of coffee. He was drinking so much that the pot was actually fresh most of the time. Tonight was the big casino and poker night at the Candlewood Center, but he wasn't going to make it, much to his grandfather's disgust. Nick knew he'd be crappy company and, more than that, he wanted to stop by Eden's place once she was finished with this damned birthday party. See if she'd thawed at all. Yeah, he'd screwed up royally, but...hell, he didn't even have an excuse.

"A couple hours. Why?"

"Just curious. And we have a problem."

"Another one?" Nick asked, settling back in his chair.

"Yeah." Daphne held out a photo, which for once wasn't a mug shot. "This is a picture of the guy that Tremont said he talked to. Ronnie Esparza. I got it from his mother." Daphne smiled. "A very sweet woman. Anyway, do you notice a problem?"

"You mean that this guy is short and chubby with black hair?"

"Uh, yeah. And we're looking for a guy who's tall and thin with long brownish hair."

"That guy could be working with Esparza." Nick huffed out a breath. "Ronnie probably doesn't have any prints on file?"

"Nope."

"Excellent," Nick said, as Marcus came into the room carrying a sheaf of papers. He cast a quick cold look in Daphne's direction, then sat at the table next to Nick.

"I chased down the VIN of the abandoned vehicle. It's registered to Colby Construction."

"I'm not familiar with it," Daphne said.

"Probably because they do no construction. If you trace the company, as I have, you'll find that it's a subsidiary of a subsidiary."

Nick waited, but Marcus didn't do his usual slow, dramatic reveal. Instead he said quietly, "Ultimately, the company is owned by Michael Ballard."

The entertainment director of the Summit Hotel in Tahoe and its sister hotel in Reno, the Cassandra—Eden's client. Nick's gut tightened. It was casino night at the Candlewood Center, which meant it was also the night of that frigging party she was giving there.

"Imagine that," Daphne said sarcastically. "Shell companies. Why on earth would he need those?"

"To launder money," Marcus said simply.

And in a display of extreme patience, which spoke to how impressed she was with Marcus's quick work tracing the vehicle, Daphne calmly replied, "I see." She glanced over at Nick and said, "What now?"

"I'll start working on a document warrant," Marcus said with an air of extreme importance, ignoring the fact that Daphne was talking to Nick. "See if we can get one with a gag order, so as not to tip Ballard off. Judge Vale owes me a favor."

"And you?" Daphne asked Nick.

"I'm going to a surprise birthday party."

He didn't want Eden anywhere near that Ballard son of a bitch without some protection. All he had to do was round up a prop or two, which was easy, since he still had a key to the Tremont Catering kitchen.

PATTY HAD JUST taken a tray out to the dining room, leaving Eden alone in the kitchen when the back door opened, startling her. She glanced up just as Nick walked in wearing a chef's jacket. Justin's jacket, if she wasn't mistaken. There was a distinctive blue dribble down the front.

She instantly put down the piping bag she'd been using and crossed to the door. "What are you doing here?" she demanded in a whisper, her heart beating triple time. "Is Justin all right?"

"He's fine. Marcus is watching him." Nick

grasped her shoulders and leaned his face close to hers. "We found the Jeep involved in Justin's accident. Traced it to a company Ballard owns."

Eden suddenly had a hard time breathing. "Michael?"

Michael, who'd sold Justin the Firebird for a ridiculously low sum of money because he knew how much her brother coveted the car? Michael, who'd joked with her in the kitchen dozens of times over the past four years?

"I want you to get through this party as soon as possible, then we'll get the hell out of here. Got it?"

Eden nodded.

"I don't want Ballard to suspect anything is wrong, because of the flight risk." But Nick wanted her safe. "Just give me a few hints how to look professional, okay?"

Eden finally found her voice. "Just...rearrange things on the trays if anyone comes in. Okay?"

Patty came back into the kitchen with a load of empty glasses. She gave a small gasp of surprise when she saw Nick. Eden put her finger to her lips and motioned her over.

"Nick's going to stay here in the kitchen. He's a temp who arrived late. Okay?"

Patty nodded, her eyes worried. "Is there some sort of trouble?"

"We hope not," he said. "But it's important none of the guests guess that anything is off. Can you treat me like one of the temps?"

"Of course," Patty said, tossing her head. "I once did community theater."

"Good." Nick smiled slightly and moved over to where Eden had been loading trays before he'd come in. "And if I tell you to do something, do it without question."

"Certainly." Patty drew in a breath and composed her features in a way that made Eden believe she'd probably been very good at community theater.

Eden went to stand beside Nick, putting appetizers onto the silver platters, her hands shaking slightly. *Michael owned the car that had hit Justin.*

Maybe it'd been stolen.

But if that was the case, then Nick probably wouldn't be here.

He leaned down and said close to her ear, "I won't let anything happen to you or your family. I promise you." He practically growled the words.

"Thank you," Eden said in a small voice, wondering if this nightmare was ever going to end, and how she'd gotten into it in the first place.

IN NICK'S MIND, this birthday party was lasting way longer than necessary. All he wanted to do was get Eden and Patty out of there without arousing Ballard's suspicions that something was off. Then they'd stash Justin away while Marcus pursued a document search warrant. Hopefully, they'd find evidence of money laundering, which would lead to a satisfying conclusion to drug traffic through the Summit.

Frosting on the cake would be nailing the guy for involvement in little Cully's murder.

Eden worked mechanically, her head down as she arranged food, heated hors d'oeuvres. Patty came and went, moving with quiet efficiency, giving no sign that anything was out of the ordinary, other than the occasional frowning glance in Nick's direction. And occasionally the hostess popped in, wearing a dress that smacked of big bucks, even to Nick's untrained eye, to flutter around and make helpful suggestions. Nick kept his head down so she couldn't see his face. People involved with drug trafficking were often familiar with both law enforcement and the members of the local drug task force. It was a matter of self-preservation. Know your enemy. But Mrs. Ballard didn't seem at all troubled by his sudden appearance, especially after Eden casually mentioned that she'd brought in a temp, just to make certain she could keep up with the demands of the guests.

"Lovely, lovely party," the woman cooed during her last kitchen visit. Eden smiled bitterly after the door closed behind her.

"I hate this," she muttered to Nick. The first words she'd said to him since they'd explained the situation to Patty.

He was about to reply when the dining-room door opened once more. But instead of Patty or Tina, a tall sandy-haired kid came into the kitchen, smiling over his shoulder as he entered the room. "Prosecco? You got it," he said. "I have a secret stash." He was still smiling as the door swung shut, then stopped dead when he saw Nick. "Uh, hi."

Nick nodded, his radar instantly up. He'd dealt with enough criminals to recognize that the kid had gone on high alert as soon as he spotted Nick, which gave him a bad feeling. He did not work undercover. Anyone who cared to do the research could easily identify him as Reno P.D.

and a drug task-force member. Had this kid done his research?

He started rearranging crackers on the plate in front of him, trying to figure how to get both Eden and Patty out of there if the shit hit the fan.

"Hi, Joshua," Eden said in a spectacularly professional tone. "Are you low on something?"

Nick watched out of the corner of his eye as Joshua shook his head, attempted a casual half smile. "No. I was just going to the garage for a sec. Private fridge out there." He nodded at Eden, then headed to the garage door next to the giant refrigerator, snagging a set of keys off the hook as he went.

"Is there a fridge in the garage?" Nick asked.

"No."

Nick dashed around the counter, veering sideways to avoid a collision with Patty. Joshua was climbing into his car, a wild look on his face as he waited for the wide electronic doors to slowly rise. He fumbled under the seat as Nick burst through the door.

Nick saw the flash of a weapon and was on the kid in an instant. Grabbing him by the collar, he yanked him out of the car and threw him sideways. The gun went flying out of his hand.

Joshua lunged back at him, trying to get to

the car to make his escape, but Nick knocked him sideways again, planting a knee in his back and wrenching one arm up high behind the kid's back.

"Call 9-1-1," he said to Patty, who stood in the doorway. Eden was only feet away from him, looking as if she'd been ready to jump in and help if necessary.

"I already have," Patty said.

"Get in here," Nick ordered. "Close the door behind you."

She quickly complied as Nick pulled the flex cuff out of his waistband and ratcheted it around Joshua Ballard's wrists. The kid grunted, but Nick had a feeling the thick walls of the garage were probably close to soundproof.

"What now?" Eden asked.

"Now you and Patty are going to leave through that open garage door and get into your van. You will drive away without looking back."

"You're staying here?" Eden asked, her face beyond pale.

"Backup is on the way."

"But—"

Headlights flashed in the driveway and Nick dropped his head in relief. Backup was here.

CHAPTER THIRTEEN

NICK AND DAPHNE paid for Cully's burial and gravestone. Marcus chipped in, too, when he heard what they were doing. The only other person attending the brief memorial they'd arranged was Cully's grandmother, who'd raised him. A woman of questionable reputation, she nevertheless cried her eyes out at the grave site. Even Marcus got a bit misty.

Daphne took his arm as they left, and Nick was left wondering who was propping up whom. One thing he was certain of was that Marcus would not be getting lucky that night.

Nick went home early in the afternoon to gear up mentally for the next few days, which were going to be hell. Big-name lawyers were already involved in the Ballard case and Nick, of course, was being personally sued for kidnapping, false arrest, battery...pretty much the gamut. He didn't care. Bring it on.

What he did care about was that he'd blown

his chance to get to know Eden better. To see if they could have developed a relationship that worked. He had a feeling that if they had met under more honest circumstances, it would have been doable.

But they hadn't and it wasn't.

How could he possibly apologize for almost getting her brother killed? And lying to her? Breaking into her office, her computers? How could she forgive him?

He was screwed. Eden valued trust, and he'd been as untrustworthy as they came. But he had learned one lesson: the end doesn't always justify the means.

The one bright point was that he had collared Cully's murderer and the guy who'd forced Justin off the road. They'd found a clear thumbprint belonging to Joshua Ballard on the visor of the Jeep that had rammed into Justin's Firebird—after he'd made a sworn statement he'd had no connection with the car whatsoever. The .38 slug resting in Cully's skull matched the gun Joshua had flashed at Nick. And it looked as if Michael Ballard was a big-time money launderer.

So Nick had that.

And not much else.

EDEN HESITATED AT the door of Nick's apartment. Gabe had given her the address without question when she'd phoned him at Candlewood. She'd had to cancel the very last cooking lesson for obvious reasons. After witnessing an attempted murder—and she had no doubt in her mind that Joshua would have shot Nick—she needed some time to deal with the emotional aftermath. Joshua was not the boy she'd once known. The Ballard family was not the family she'd thought she'd known. Except for Tina, who seemed to be as bewildered as she was at what had happened.

Eden had promised Gabe, though, that she would give a new set of cooking lessons in the future. Gabe gruffly told her she'd better, because he thought he might have left his wallet in a drawer there.

Finally, she lifted her hand and knocked on Nick's door, since there was no buzzer. The sound echoed hollowly, as if no one was home. She was about to knock again when she heard movement inside and her nerves jumped.

Nick opened the door and her first thought was that he looked like hell. Dark circles surrounded his eyes and his face was paler than usual. Her first impulse was to ask, "Are you all right?" But instead she said, "I want the story."

He drew back, a perplexed look chasing across his face. "What story?"

"I want to know exactly why you did everything you did. I want to know the reasons, and I think you owe me that."

For one very long minute she thought he was going to say no. Then he stepped back abruptly and Eden walked into his dimly lit apartment. There were empty beer bottles on the coffee table and a suit jacket tossed over the back of a tan recliner, but other than that, the place was Spartan. Kind of a spick-and-span man cave with a few photos on the wall, a coffee table, sofa and television.

He waved toward the sofa and Eden sat, her knees close together, her hands clasped in her lap. Nick did not sit down. He stood next to the recliner, his posture tense. That worked, because Eden wanted some distance between them while she heard "the story."

"There was this kid named Cully."

Quite possibly the last thing she'd expected him to say.

"Cully," she repeated.

"Yes. I didn't know his full name until a few days ago, when he was buried. Randall C. McCullers." Nick's mouth worked for a moment.

Not as if he were fighting emotion, but as if he were trying to come up with the words. The right words to convey what he needed to say.

Because he needed for her to understand.

Which made Eden wonder if she was important to him, just as Justin had insisted. If so, then they had so much to work through.

She sat very still, watching, waiting for him to continue.

Finally Nick rubbed a hand over the back of his neck. "He was a CI—a confidential informant—that fed Daphne and me information about the drug traffic in the Lake Tahoe area. He wasn't very old."

"How old?" Eden asked quietly.

"About the same age as Joshua Ballard," Nick said with an edge to his voice. "Who I think killed him."

"So this was a murder investigation?" That at least helped make what had happened more acceptable.

"We didn't know for sure what had happened to him when we started. He'd set up a meeting to give us information he'd gotten about how the drug money from the Tahoe Summit was laundered. He never showed and we never heard from him again."

Eden clasped her hands even tighter. And her brother worked there. Had worked there for several years.

Nick propped his forearms on the back of the tan chair, lightly touching his fingertips together. "The only thing we knew was that a business in Reno was involved. The only person in the Summit with a small-business tie was Justin."

All right. That she could see.

Nick tapped the ends of his fingers together in a distracted manner. "We know now the business involved was actually Colby Construction. Owned by Michael Ballard."

"But before you knew that, you needed to find out whether Justin was laundering drug money."

"Yes." Nick met her eyes, his gaze hard, his mouth tight.

"So you, what? Broke into our records?"

He nodded and started to speak, but Eden cut him off, holding up a hand to silence him. "You know what? I don't want to know the ins and outs of the espionage."

"You said you wanted answers."

"The espionage is more of a technicality." She dropped her chin for a moment.

"I was trying to break a case. Stop drugs. Find a murderer."

"Worthy causes," Eden agreed. "And I was collateral damage." She unclasped her hands and rubbed the palms over the tops of her thighs. "I feel broken, Nick." The words came out in a whisper.

"I know."

She glanced up then, shaking her hair back. "I don't think you do."

"I know broken." His voice was harsh. Adamant. "I've been broken…hell, I'm still broken." He spoke the last words so quietly that she barely heard them.

"Nick…"

He stepped away from the chair where he'd been rooted since starting his explanation, stopping a few feet from her. "I'm not going to ask you for forgiveness. But I am going to explain something else. I lied to you time and time again, but I never lied to you with my body. Or my heart, for that matter. I hated doing what I did. I felt justified." He drew in a long breath. "And I may have been, since it ultimately solved a crime. But I will forever regret the way this turned out."

"And now it's too late." It was a statement. A challenging one. Eden stood, acting on sheer instinct. "Do you know how many things have felt one way to me and turned out to be the opposite?"

"Quite a lot lately," he said on a bitter note.

"So I ask myself how I'm supposed to know what's real."

"Sometimes you can't."

"And sometimes you can." Eden stepped forward and took his face in her hands, her body instinctively reacting to the warm feel of his skin beneath her palms. Slowly, she pulled his head down to kiss his lips lightly, as she'd done the very first time she'd ever kissed him.

"How does that feel?" she asked when she raised her head. "Does it feel real?"

"Eden...don't do this."

"And this." She kissed him again, her tongue touching his upper lip. As before, he fought it. For a few seconds. Then he groaned and hauled her against him. "Feels real, doesn't it?" She touched his chest, where his heart beat beneath her palm. "And here. It feels real here."

He nodded without speaking, still holding her in his arms as she reached up to touch his forehead. "Which makes me think it's real here. I almost died when Joshua Ballard pulled that gun."

"Me, too. I thought I was going to lose you."

Eden leaned her head against his shoulder.

"How long does it take to rebuild trust?" he asked in a low voice, his arms closing around her more tightly.

"I'm thinking more about starting fresh."

"Is that possible?" Nick murmured against her hair. "Considering all that's happened?"

She leaned back to look him in the eye. "Everything in me is telling me to try. Telling me that I'll be worse off if I don't." She felt tears welling, but blinked them back. "That's why I don't want to walk away. I'm not done with you yet."

He drew her against him, holding her tightly, and Eden pressed a soft kiss to the side of his neck.

"No easy fix, Nick, but I want to try."

She felt him smile against her temple. "That sounds real."

EPILOGUE

Six months later

"How do I look?" Gabe asked Eden.

She reached to straighten the already straight lapels of his lightweight sports jacket. He'd suggested a tie, but she'd squelched that idea, saying a tie in the heat of an Indian summer was not the most relaxed look—even inside an air-conditioned airport.

Nick leaned against the wall next to the lobby newsstand, smiling slightly. Gabe took a few nervous paces, all the while keeping his eyes on the escalator leading down from the airport security area and the flight gates.

"You two can go, you know," he said suddenly.

Nick pushed off from the wall. "Do you *want* us to go?"

Gabe shoved his hands into his pockets. "Uh... maybe you could kind of hover in the distance."

"So we can't hear if she tells you to go to hell?"

"Stop it, Nick." Eden smiled at Gabe. "She isn't flying up from southern Nevada to tell you to go to hell."

"You don't know Bonita. She just might." Gabe said it with a mixture of pride and anxiety. "This is killing me—"

"Granddad," Nick said, "you guys were together for how many years?"

"Five. But—" Gabe broke off abruptly and his mouth went tight for a moment. "There she is," he murmured.

And indeed, there she was. Eden recognized Bonita from the photos, a trim blonde woman in her early seventies with angular features. She was near the top of the escalator, carrying an oversize white bag and wearing skinny-legged pants and a fashionable dark green tunic. When she saw Gabe, her lips parted and then she started walking down the moving steps, squeezing past the two people in front of her.

Gabe started forward, but had only made it a few yards before she threw herself into his arms. He stood stiffly for a few seconds, then his arms closed around her and he held her, rocking her gently as the people moved around them.

"I didn't think you...you sounded so uncertain..." Gabe muttered.

"I had to *make* certain," she said. "I wasn't going to come until I was certain."

"And now?"

"I'm here," she said.

Nick nudged Eden and when she looked up at him, he smiled and then held out his hand. Eden slipped her fingers into his and he squeezed them. "Time to leave the lovebirds alone."

"I thought we were their ride."

He shook his head. "Only if she told him to go to hell. Granddad has a cab waiting."

"So we're just here—"

"To make sure he looked all right," Nick said with a smile. The automatic door opened and he and Eden walked out into the unseasonably warm October day.

"Think it'll work out?" she asked as they crossed the street to the parking garage. Gabe had been very upfront about the mistakes he'd made, obviously in hopes that Nick wouldn't follow suit. Eden loved him because of it. Gabe was becoming the grandfather she'd never had and she wanted him to be happy, so Bonita had better be careful.

"They've communicated for six months. They

may have had some shaky times in the past, but you know what?" Nick stopped next to his SUV and pulled out the keys.

"What?" Eden asked with a half smile.

He settled his hands on her waist and leaned his face close to hers, looking at her in a way that made her catch her breath. "I know from personal experience that it's possible to overcome a shaky start. To learn and grow and build something good from something bad."

"You weren't bad."

"But I wasn't good, either." He kissed her lightly, but with the unspoken promise of better things to come. Soon. "All I can say is thank you for giving me a second chance."

Eden pulled his lips back to hers, ignoring the couple dragging suitcases toward the exit behind them. "And all I can say is thank you for taking it."

* * * * *

HEART & HOME

Heartwarming romances where love can
happen right when you least expect it.

Harlequin®
Super Romance

You can find more information on upcoming Harlequin® titles,
free excerpts and more at www.HarlequinInsideRomance.com.

HSRCNM0112

REQUEST YOUR FREE BOOKS!
2 FREE NOVELS PLUS 2 FREE GIFTS!

Harlequin® Super Romance®

Exciting, emotional, unexpected!

YES! Please send me 2 FREE Harlequin® Superromance® novels and my 2 FREE gifts (gifts are worth about $10). After receiving them, if I don't wish to receive any more books, I can return the shipping statement marked "cancel." If I don't cancel, I will receive 6 brand-new novels every month and be billed just $4.69 per book in the U.S. or $5.24 per book in Canada. That's a saving of at least 15% off the cover price! It's quite a bargain! Shipping and handling is just 50¢ per book in the U.S. and 75¢ per book in Canada.* I understand that accepting the 2 free books and gifts places me under no obligation to buy anything. I can always return a shipment and cancel at any time. Even if I never buy another book, the two free books and gifts are mine to keep forever.

135/336 HDN FC6T

Name _____ (PLEASE PRINT)

Address _____ Apt. #

City _____ State/Prov. _____ Zip/Postal Code

Signature (if under 18, a parent or guardian must sign)

Mail to the **Reader Service**:
IN U.S.A.: P.O. Box 1867, Buffalo, NY 14240-1867
IN CANADA: P.O. Box 609, Fort Erie, Ontario L2A 5X3

Not valid for current subscribers to Harlequin Superromance books.
**Are you a current subscriber to Harlequin Superromance books
and want to receive the larger-print edition?**
Call 1-800-873-8635 or visit www.ReaderService.com.

* Terms and prices subject to change without notice. Prices do not include applicable taxes. Sales tax applicable in N.Y. Canadian residents will be charged applicable taxes. Offer not valid in Quebec. This offer is limited to one order per household. All orders subject to credit approval. Credit or debit balances in a customer's account(s) may be offset by any other outstanding balance owed by or to the customer. Please allow 4 to 6 weeks for delivery. Offer available while quantities last.

Your Privacy—The Reader Service is committed to protecting your privacy. Our Privacy Policy is available online at www.ReaderService.com or upon request from the Reader Service.

We make a portion of our mailing list available to reputable third parties that offer products we believe may interest you. If you prefer that we not exchange your name with third parties, or if you wish to clarify or modify your communication preferences, please visit us at www.ReaderService.com/consumerschoice or write to us at Reader Service Preference Service, P.O. Box 9062, Buffalo, NY 14269. Include your complete name and address.

HSRI I

New York Times *and* USA TODAY *bestselling author Maya Banks presents book three in her miniseries* PREGNANCY & PASSION.

TEMPTED BY HER INNOCENT KISS

Available March 2012 from Harlequin Desire!

There came a time in a man's life when he knew he was well and truly caught. Devon Carter stared down at the diamond ring nestled in velvet and acknowledged that this was one such time. He snapped the lid closed and shoved the box into the breast pocket of his suit.

He had two choices. He could marry Ashley Copeland and fulfill his goal of merging his company with Copeland Hotels, thus creating the largest, most exclusive line of resorts in the world, or he could refuse and lose it all.

Put in that light, there wasn't much he could do except pop the question.

The doorman to his Manhattan high-rise apartment hurried to open the door as Devon strode toward the street. He took a deep breath before ducking into his car, and the driver pulled into traffic.

Tonight was the night. All of his careful wooing, the countless dinners, kisses that started brief and casual and became more breathless—all a lead-up to tonight. Tonight his seduction of Ashley Copeland would be complete, and then he'd ask her to marry him.

He shook his head as the absurdity of the situation hit him for the hundredth time. Personally, he thought William Copeland was crazy for forcing his daughter down Devon's throat.

Ashley was a sweet enough girl, but Devon had no desire

to marry anyone.

William had other plans. He'd told Devon that Ashley had no head for the family business. She was too softhearted, too naive. So he'd made Ashley part of the deal. The catch? Ashley wasn't to know of it. Which meant Devon was stuck playing stupid games.

Ashley was supposed to think this was a grand love match. She was a starry-eyed woman who preferred her animal-rescue foundation over board meetings, charts and financials for Copeland Hotels.

If she ever found out the truth, she wouldn't take it well.

And hell, he couldn't blame her.

But no matter the reason for his proposal, before the night was over, she'd have no doubts that she belonged to him.

What will happen when Devon marries Ashley?
Find out in Maya Banks's passionate new novel
TEMPTED BY HER INNOCENT KISS
Available March 2012 from Harlequin Desire!

HDEXP0312